THE CURSE OF
PORTER'S HOLLOW

Yvonne Schuchart

Print ISBN: 978-1-64649-018-9
Ebook ISBN: 978-1-64649-019-6

 Year of the Book
135 Glen Avenue
Glen Rock, PA 17327

Library of Congress Control Number: 2019913382

DEDICATION

This third book in the Porter's Hollow series
is dedicated once again to my readers.
Thank you for giving me your time.

Yvonne
Schuchart
7/22/23

ACKNOWLEDGMENTS

The release of a new book is like the birth of a baby. You hold that beautiful living thing in your hands and you think, *Wow, did I really produce this?* But like childbirth and labor, you don't get through the production of a book alone. There are always others who deserve credit for helping you through.

Again, I have to thank my husband, Earl, for being there for me, encouraging me to believe in myself and my strengths and abilities.

Of course, without Demi Stevens of Year of the Book, patient coach and avid cheerleader, and my personal book midwife, this bun would have stayed in the oven. I went through a lot of changes these past two years that threatened to keep me from getting this book done. Indeed, it is later to its birth than it was meant to be and for that I apologize to my readers.

I have to say a big thank you also to Kimberly Albert and Dena Tyndall for taking the time to proofread and tidy up this baby's little messes.

As always, I appreciate the comments and thoughts of readers. I've been encouraged by the reviews, critiques, and responses to the previous books in the Porter's Hollow series.

And finally, once again, I thank my readers for the time they take to read my work.

"The whole course of human history may depend on a change of heart in one solitary and even humble individual—for it is in the solitary mind and soul of the individual that the battle between good and evil is waged and ultimately won or lost."

—M. Scott Peck, *The Road Less Traveled*, 1978

CHAPTER 1

Porter's Hollow, Grassy Creek, NC
October 1968

Scrabbling around under the cabin porch looking for eggs, Laurie Allen Porter's hand gently rubbed a smooth surface. She didn't want to crush them. Always cool and oh-so-fragile, the hard-to-the touch surface held her fancy. She liked to watch when the chicks hatched, pecking their way through the delicate shell, emerging wet looking, scrawny and shaky. Using her right hand to wipe fiercely at the dust in her eyes, she finally managed to peer into the darkness.

Too big for an egg, the smooth white surface her hand rested on was broken by two large, dark holes staring at her. Laurie opened her mouth to scream but nothing came out. Her whole body froze, except for her eyes. On their own they traveled down from the black holes to the tattered, dirty blue dress. A bony hand protruded from the rotting fabric, an arm wrapped around a filthy baby doll with decomposing artificial blonde hair.

Her limbs finally loosened, and she jerked away and scrambled backward on her belly.

If she'd stayed and turned the bony head the other way, she'd have seen the large dark crack splitting the skull. But she was only eight, and not so brave as all that. Not so brave at all.

CHAPTER 2

Grassy Creek, NC
Tuesday, November 16, 2010

The Toyota Corolla rounded a bend in the dirt lane, cautiously navigating the ancient, muddy tire ruts. Its headlamps created twin spirals of light in an otherwise velvet black night. Laura rubbed her burning, gritty eyes and yawned. Shifting position and pressing her shoulder blades together, she stretched her neck, but as she settled back against the seat, she caught a glimpse of movement on the road ahead. Too big to be a dog, or even a deer, whatever it was cut across the road and disappeared into the brush about a hundred yards away. A tingle coursed through Laura's body all the way to her scalp.

She feathered the gas pedal, left foot poised over the clutch, her chest rising and falling in quick shallow breaths, heart thumping in the soft jugular notch at the base of her throat. Then she heard it, the familiar rumble of an ATV with no tailpipe. In the next instant the vehicle lurched back onto the road and spun around to face her, coming to a dead stop. Laura dropped the Corolla out of gear and braked, waiting.

A pair of closely spaced headlights flipped on. *What the...* Was he seriously going to play chicken—on a four-wheeler? Neither one moved for endless seconds, until Laura heard the ATV's tires digging dirt and saw it lunge forward, mud flying in the backdrop of the red tail light's glow.

Laura slammed the clutch to the floor, jerked the gear shift into reverse and spun wheels backwards as fast as she could maneuver on the rough farm lane. Silt, sludge, and gravel flew, pinging off the car, hitting the windows. The four-wheeler's headlamps grew ominously as it shot straight at her, like it was being driven by a demon from hell.

The careening four-wheeler swerved and went off the road, barely missing the Toyota's bumper. Splattering muck across the windshield and obscuring Laura's view of the rider, it rumbled by and was gone.

She stopped and checked the rearview mirror, watching as the ATV disappeared. Breathing hard, hands shaking, she finally got the car into first gear, but her foot slipped, and she gunned the gas pedal causing her tires to catch on the ridge running through the middle of the dirt road. The bottom dropped out of her stomach as the Toyota lurched, but she swerved back into the rutted tracks and slowed, checking the rearview again. No sign of the battered four-wheeler.

It could only be one person.

Laura's hands were still trembling when she pulled into the farmhouse driveway. The lights were on and Aunt Hattie stepped out. The screen door closed with a bang that made Laura jump. The elderly woman held up a withered arm, shielding her eyes from the glare of the porch light. *Thank God, she's okay.* The tawny-haired Certified Nursing Assistant stood in the doorway behind Aunt Hattie, smiling and waving. *No trouble here.*

Laura turned the car off and remained at the wheel. She couldn't trust her legs to carry her yet. Her whole body weak, she laid her head on her hands, clutching the steering wheel white-knuckled. She still couldn't figure out how he could possibly be alive, even though they'd never found his body. It had been carried off by the most vile, evil creature she'd ever encountered—some sort of spirit beast in the form of a large black wolf standing upright on its thick hind legs. She wouldn't have believed it if she hadn't seen it for herself... if she hadn't smelled its feral stink, and felt its hot breath on her face.

But what had Loy been trying to do just now? Run her off the road and kill her? Did he even know it was her? Did the creature have control of him? Had he been here at Aunt Hattie's?

She took a deep cleansing breath and stepped out of her car. Road weariness, and the drain of fear and spent adrenaline pulled on her like gravity. She looked up at the white clapboard, emotion welling in her eyes.

In her heart, Laura had always harbored a passion for this place, though as a child she'd been forced to hide her feelings. Her mother had hated it. Robey had even gone so far as to move them both to Pennsylvania, breaking all ties with family. It had taken Laura's determination to go back and look for her father to get Robey to reconcile with the past. And now, both she and Laura's father, Glen Porter, were gone.

But these high mountains, deep hollows and lush forests felt like home, and the white-haired woman standing there on the front porch was second only in Laura's heart to her own daughter.

Aunt Hattie tilted her head, peering into the vehicle, and took a step down while Laura gathered her wits enough to clamber out of the Toyota on rubbery legs. She gave the area a quick once over and hurried to move them all inside. Closing and locking the front door behind her, Laura turned and wrapped her aunt in a hug so tight the other woman grunted.

Hattie patted Laura's back. "Goodness sakes, child, it's barely over a week. But I missed you, too."

Laura had rushed through the arrangements on her house and managed to come back earlier than she'd thought possible. But she'd fretted almost constantly about her aunt. Seeing how frail the woman looked didn't put her mind any more at ease. Guilt still plagued her over all those lost years. She should have come back long ago and taken part in Hattie's life... now Laura worried she might not have much time left.

"Well, I missed you more." Laura managed a smile though her insides were still churning. She considered whether to tell Hattie about her encounter with the four-wheeler, but the elderly woman was recovering from an aggressive bladder infection. She'd only been allowed to convalesce at home on the condition she take it easy and have someone there with her every day—which is where the CNA came in.

Hattie smiled, eyes shining. "Well, I sure am glad you're back. You sell that house a' yours yet?"

"Oh, no, not this quick. The realtor will take care of showing it. Of course, I'll have to go back a couple of times to finish up with things, but hopefully only a day or two at a time."

"Well, you come on in and set down to the table. Have a cup a' tea and some cookies. I know it's late, but I want to hear 'bout your momma's funeral. Still wish I could a' been there with you."

Laura tucked an arm around Hattie's waist as they walked to the kitchen, observing her closely. The other woman was always thin and wiry, but she looked, and felt, like she'd lost weight. Hattie's sparkling, snow-white hair had dulled and showed signs of yellowing at the temples. She had a sallow, hollow-eyed look. Laura couldn't bear the thought of losing her so soon after reconnecting. It might be selfish, but she longed for more time to share the memories they'd missed out on, time to recover those they'd shared so long ago, time to add new ones to their story.

The CNA, who had quietly disappeared into the kitchen earlier, interrupted her thoughts to go over Hattie's medical notes, while her aunt poured the tea.

Cayley O'Donnell, an Ashe County native whose thick auburn hair and light smattering of freckles gave away her Irish roots as much as her name did, sat down next to Laura and flipped open her journal. The young woman was dressed neatly in trim-fit burgundy scrubs. She was meticulous with her patient's records, but her genuine concern for Aunt Hattie was what impressed Laura most. Her brother, Tom, had recommended the girl. He had said she was a longtime member of the Ashe County Baptist Church where he was pastor. Grew up there, in fact, though Tom had only come to know her when he'd returned home and taken over the pastorate. She'd been in her teens then. Apparently she had moved away for a time just out of high school, but had returned a few years ago with her certification and started in-home care through a local agency.

Thinking of all that reminded Laura how strange it felt on her tongue, and in her head, to call Tom her brother. Half-brother, actually, but she'd never known about him until she'd come back here in search of the father they shared. In truth it was no stranger than encountering forgotten uncles, an ancient but living grandmother, and newly acquired psychic visions the likes of which might cause others to think her crazy.

In all the chaos, however, it was comforting to hear Aunt Hattie's prognosis was good. She was still taking antibiotics, but recent blood tests showed the infection was almost gone. After Cayley explained the medication schedule, she said, "I'll take the morning tomorrow to catch up on some things, then I'll be back tomorrow afternoon. I'm normally scheduled to come in every day around 10:00 and leave just after dinner, 'round 6:00 or 7:00. I'll always call to check on her first thing in the morning though, long as she's in my care." The young woman had been staying with Aunt Hattie 24/7 while Laura was gone. "But I can be available for other hours you might need." Cayley lowered her voice and leaned in then. "We need to make sure she eats regular, gets lots of rest and takes her meds. Older folks tend to forget to do the little things when they aren't well, and those little things add up to make it harder and harder for them to take care of themselves. But with a bit of help, most can spring back and do well."

Laura once again silently thanked her brother for introducing Cayley to them. The two already had an easy rapport despite their age difference. The CNA had a compassionate face and gentle eyes. She was genuinely concerned for her patient. That alone gave Laura reason to like the girl.

After seeing Cayley out and locking the front door, Laura watched Hattie's face a moment. "So, how are you feeling?"

"Better. Least wise, I can't complain. But..." The elderly woman paused, lips pursed.

"What? Did the doctor say something else?"

"No," she said. "No, it's just—well—I still get confused some now and then. I'm not used to feelin' so muddled."

"Oh." Laura stopped and looked the older woman over again. "You were awfully sick. It might take a while to get back to normal."

Hattie lifted her chin and smiled. "I s'pose you're right." She pressed her mouth in a thin line and shook her head. Then she drew a breath and changed the conversation. "So, tell me 'bout the funeral. You had a preacher speak, didn't you?"

The two women talked until Hattie yawned so big, guilt pushed Laura to her feet. She reached to help the elderly woman up from her chair and linked arms with her as they climbed the stairs. "I've kept you up way too late. You need your rest, and we can talk again tomorrow—and the next day—and every day."

Before she laid down, Aunt Hattie put a thin, withered hand to Laura's face and smiled. "It's gonna be real nice havin' you here."

Laura made sure the elderly woman was settled in for the night before heading back down to the living room. Picking up the handset, she dialed the sheriff's number. She didn't realize she was holding her breath until hearing a click on the other end of the line.

"Hello?" Blaine Wilson answered in a southern drawl husky with sleep.

Laura's face warmed at the sound. "Hey, it's me. Sorry if I woke you."

"No," he yawned into the receiver, "no, it's fine. Are you here in North Carolina?"

"I would've waited to call, but..." she sighed and answered, "...I practically got run off the farm lane by a four-wheeler." She paused a moment before adding, "Loy's."

"What?" His voice cleared in an instant. "Were you hurt?"

"No, I'm fine. I just thought you should know, since you're looking for him."

"So, I was right. He is alive. And kicking."

"I'm sorry to bother you this time of night..."

"It's no problem." He stifled another yawn. "I can be there in about twenty minutes."

"No, I don't want you to keep running over here at every little thing that happens. We're fine."

"Alright, but I'll have the night shift deputy swing by soon as we hang up." He paused before asking, "Laura, are you okay?"

"I'll be fine."

He sighed heavily into the phone. "Okay. But I'll be there in the morning after I check in at the office, say around 7:30 or 8:00?" He paused, then added, "And don't worry, I'll figure this all out eventually."

There it was again, that condescending tone he sometimes slipped into. She almost blurted out, *"What makes you think I need anyone to figure things out for me?"* She rubbed her neck and stifled a yawn. She should be grateful to have someone watching out for them, and she was. Yet sometimes Blaine's demeanor gave her the impression he thought of her as a weak, witless female. Instead she answered, "I will. Thanks."

After Laura hung up, she sat with Aunt Hattie's old shotgun across her lap, waiting for the deputy, setting it down only after she was sure it was him on the porch.

Adam Richardson was lean and lanky, his jaw angular, his demeanor always so official. But his soft brown eyes and almost shy smile gave away his real personality.

"Ma'am," the deputy tipped his hat to her as he stepped inside. "I mean, Miss Laura." His face colored self-consciously. "It's good to see you again. Hope Miss Hattie's doin' well."

He shifted nervously from one foot to the other as he appeared to attempt to see around Laura into the sitting room.

"She's doing well, thank you." Laura smiled in response. Not sure she was interpreting his concern correctly, she added, "But she's gone up to bed now."

"Glad to hear it." He settled his hat back down on his head tight. "I guess Miss Cayley's gone for the night then?" The deputy glanced around again.

"Yes. She'll be back tomorrow, late morning." Laura smiled inwardly, noting the distinct cloud of disappointment that crossed the young man's face.

"I've checked around. Nothing out there now. I'll run by here again later. Stop by in the morning too, ma'am." He nodded and backed out the door.

"Thank you again, Adam."

She closed the door with a gentle thud and glanced up the stairs, but her aunt hadn't stirred. Hattie Perkins was Laura's first responsibility, and the main reason she'd decided to move to North Carolina. Of course, there was the way she and Blaine had left things hanging between them. But judging by what had happened in the caves up in the mountain last week, and the harrowing standoff on the road, it was certain the next thing on the list had to be dealing, once and for all, with the Porter family curse.

CHAPTER 3

Crashing through the woods, swerving around trees, careening left and right, Loy Porter drove with the devil at his heels.

Miss Laurie was in danger. He'd been watching Miss Hattie's, waiting for her. He needed to see her, talk to her, tell her he would keep the beast from hurting her. He'd promised Glen. No matter what, he wouldn't let the beast take his little Laurie.

And now she was back. It was her in the little silver car. He hadn't meant to scare her. He just wanted to see her and make sure she was safe. Tell her he'd watch out for her—always.

But that devil beast got into his mind again telling him awful things. Sent him flying right at her, but he wouldn't hurt Miss Laurie, not for all the world. Though, if he hadn't jerked the wheel at the last second, he'd a' crashed right through her window. He had to find a way to get rid of the creature once and for all. And if he couldn't...

He suddenly swerved hard to avoid a rock and caught a big root, bumping the four-wheeler up in the air, slamming it down hard, jarring his teeth. His eyes burned and he couldn't swallow right. His mouth was all dry, his tongue three sizes too big. "Aaaah!" His mouth flew open and he hollered as the ATV popped over a log.

The world around him began to glow red. His head was splitting, he could feel his body swell, and he was so hot inside he thought he'd go up in flames any minute.

"No, no, no, no, no!" he cried aloud. Taking a hand off the handlebars, he smacked his own head several times, but lost control of the ATV. Grabbing wildly, he ducked to miss an overhanging branch and leaned at the same time. His own weight tipped the four-wheeler, sending him slamming into a tree. The last thing he saw before his eyes was Laura's beautiful face, afraid and crying.

CHAPTER 4

Rolling over for the umpteenth time in the last hour, Laura readjusted the covers and closed her eyes, tucking the back of one hand into the crook of her neck. Her mind had drifted close to unconsciousness more than once, but each time, in that last lingering moment before sleep, something caused her eyes to snap open.

An eerily familiar sound, a faint cry, like a young woman pleading. Laura hadn't been able to make out the words, but she sensed the girl's desperation.

The strange psychic awareness first came to Laura in dreams, right after her father, Glen Porter, called asking her to come to North Carolina. She'd thought he was dead. But poor health, desperation, and loneliness drove him to contact his only daughter. His love child.

When he died from a bullet meant for her, the dreams became waking visions. She'd thought they'd stopped once she exposed the truth behind Lottie Edwards' death, but it wasn't long before they returned. And they still came to her, even after their murderer—her uncle, Curry Porter—was finally caught and killed. They wanted more from her, and now, at last, she believed she knew why—the curse brought on by her great, great grandfather.

James Delaney Porter had used his own mother's hoodoo practices for evil, calling up a vile spirit to curse his neighbors for rejecting him and his family, but the being apparently turned its focus on James and his descendants instead. Which meant as long as that demon creature roamed Porter's Hollow, Laura would continue to be visited by its tormented victims, and her family would live in danger of its influence—even if she was the only one who believed the whole impossible story.

But right now, she was too tired to respond to the visions. She needed to unwind and get some sleep. She had learned how to shut them out for short periods. If she simply changed her thoughts, moved herself physically and refused to pay attention to them, they would leave her alone—but not indefinitely. Sooner or later they found a way to communicate.

Feet hitting the cold floor, Laura shivered and reached for a pair of thick socks. Then she pulled an oversized flannel shirt on over her long tee. In the dim glow filtering through the doorway from a nightlight in the hall, she sifted through the boxes she had yet to unpack until she located the bottle of Sangria. She'd brought along a set of large-globe wine glasses and a wing-style corkscrew as well. Collecting these, she padded down the stairs to the kitchen to pour a glass, then settled on the sofa in the living room. Or as Aunt Hattie called it, the sitting room.

She opened a book she'd gotten from her newfound half-brother Tom, a man known to most people around here as the Reverend Cecil Thomas Honeywell. She flipped through the heavy tome on the history of demonology to a section that pictured artists' renderings of various demons and the forms they may take.

She focused on one creature, studying its near human body, yet more wolf-like head, teeth and claws. She noted the eyes in the illustration were evil looking, but not the same as the creature she'd faced. That one's eyes had been—intelligent—knowing. It was as if the thing she'd witnessed was aware of what it was and knew exactly what it was doing.

It was not a dumb, vicious beast. It was a sentient being. Its eyes had bored into her, full of hatred and malice. It knew her somehow. Its look was a leering, suggestive reproach, as if it knew she was guilty of some wicked, horrible transgression. It intended to have her; she was sure of that. She didn't know exactly what it had in mind, but she knew it wanted her to suffer. It wanted her fear, and she sensed it wanted her blood. Yet, there was something else in its gaze, something she couldn't quite identify, something accusatory, condemning—and delighted.

Laura's focus turned inward, and though her eyes stayed aimed at the artist's picture, she no longer saw it with clear consciousness. In its place, the creature she knew took shape—its glittering yellow fangs, its burning red eyes, its wiry black hair, all came into focus. A feral odor stung her nose for a few seconds, then suddenly she could hardly breathe. A heavy musty smell overwhelmed her and when the thing reached for her, she jumped.

Her vision cleared in an instant. But the hand that touched her was not the horrible, clawed, demon paw. The hand that brushed her forearm, or rather left its cold impression, was a pale, white hand—delicate, but scarred. Streaked with old wounds that had dried over but never healed, and it was still extended. The apparition was yet another young woman. All of them so far had been about the same average to thin build, roughly the same age— early teens to possibly mid-twenties. The hair was different though in various shades of blonde, brunette, and black, but all appeared to have been beaten, ravaged, and stabbed. Their torn, bloodied clothing and gaping wounds suggesting they'd suffered vile tortures.

She still didn't know how many there were, or if they were all her Uncle Curry's victims. She'd never tried to count their numbers, and other than the Down Syndrome girl, Lottie Edwards, she'd never been able to identify any. Yet, she felt she owed it to them somehow. Like she had to come back here to Porter's Hollow—for them—not her father. And another thought filled her consciousness... she had to be the one. Laura had to find the truth and finish this herself, and the idea chilled her to the core.

The girl stood watching Laura, no longer crying audibly, but tears streaked her pale, dirty face. The spirits never actually spoke to her, but sometimes she would hear their haunting cries, and Lottie Edwards had once mouthed a message to Laura, wanting her to come back to the hollow. Yet now this girl simply stood staring, almost glaring at Laura with reproach. Something in her expression made Laura feel she *ought* to know what the enigmatic wraith wanted.

The apparition lifted her chin and raised an eyebrow with a scornful look. Then she turned her head left and Laura followed with her eyes. The forest stretched before her, dying leaves thick on the ground between the tall bare trees. The odor of wet decay wafted on the air along with a cold, damp mist. The ghostly figure walked into the haze, stopping to glance back several times, the look of disdain still evident in her features. Laura followed unwillingly—something about this vision felt wrong.

The path turned into the trail at Porter's Hollow beyond Aunt Hattie's. The wraithlike figure paused at the ramshackle remains of the Dillon's cabin, where Laura had found Lottie Edwards' skeleton in the cold dark space under the porch so long ago. Stopping to run a pale, delicate hand down the post at the corner where Laura had been so traumatized, the apparition practically sneered at her. Then, swirling her hand around the support, the young woman turned and moved on yet again.

Time and space in these visions were jumbled and disproportionate. The vision took Laura to her Granny Beulah's home, but not as it looked now. The whitewashed paint was fresh, the boards all in place. The nebulous spirit continued around the side of the building and stopped, turning her scornful gaze on Laura then back at the base of the house.

Breathing shallow, her vision blurring, Laura backed away. The ghostly figure stared hard, brazen anger in her expression. Again, that sense that Laura ought to know... something... overwhelmed her. She shook her head and backed away further, not realizing she'd been on her feet in the sitting room until she bumped into the end table. She dropped to the floor and hid her face in her hands.

CHAPTER 5

October 1968

"You hurt her." Laurie Allen pooched her lip out, frowning hard at her Uncle Curry. "You hurt that little girl, didn't you?"

Curry stepped in close, glaring down at her, his face all twisted, dark, and angry. He grabbed her upper arm and turned, dragging her around the side of the house. "Time you learned," he mumbled, yanking open the root cellar door. Flipping on a flashlight, he wrapped one arm around her middle and carried her down into the darkness.

It was cold, the air smelled bad, and the dampness made her shiver hard. Curry slammed her butt down on the cold, slimy, hard packed dirt floor—packed so hard and walked over so much it had a shiny smoothness to it, making her think of the skin of a dragon. And it smelled like she imagined dragons would, even though she knew they weren't real. But she feared some monsters did exist, and she was sure her Uncle Curry was one of the worst kind.

"You gonna learn, little missy. You don't go accusin' your elders of things you don't know nothin' 'bout."

Laurie watched him disappear through the circle of light created by the opening above. Then the cellar door slammed and she was swallowed in blackness.

CHAPTER 6

The smooth motion of the ladder-backed rocking chair on the front porch had Laura drifting into hypnotic reverie. Breakfast was over, Hattie was upstairs resting, and the deputy had returned to take a walk around the place, then stationed himself near the barn waiting for the sheriff to arrive.

Her subconscious noted a strange odor floating on the cool breeze. It made Laura crinkle her nose, but she stayed on the porch rocking. Most likely a dead coon or groundhog somewhere nearby.

Laura's thoughts drifted to the mountains above Porter's Hollow and the cold damp caves. Curry had kidnapped and held both Laura and Robey in those dark caverns. The man was a crazed serial killer who claimed he was driven to murder by a demon—with her own mother his latest victim. And the police were still trying to identify the other remains they'd found in those blue mason jars. Laura struggled to wrap her mind around the reality. Biting tears stung her eyes, but she continued the reflex rocking of the chair.

The reds, yellows, and deepening browns of autumn blurred. A chilly breeze stirred the leaves on the ground and in the trees, while the shagbark hickory to the left of the porch shuddered in a sudden gust. She tucked her hands into the pockets of her hoodie. The cool, damp air chilled her to the bone, but she kept rocking.

A little blonde-haired girl in a tattered blue dress, face battered and bloody, her head tilted, eyes silently pleading for help, filled Laura's mind. Lottie Edwards had been the only face from her dreams and visions that she could remember clearly—until last night.

The last time the specter of Lottie appeared was in the cave, standing by, watching as the beast attacked, and somehow moving the shotgun within reach. Until then, Laura had no idea the dead could move objects.

But Lottie no longer came to her in actual form. It was the other one now, the girl with the long dark hair who looked so accusingly at Laura. She couldn't shake the feeling she should know this girl and whatever had happened to her, but it made no sense. Still the girl's expression created an unsettled feeling in the pit of Laura's stomach. The thought of her now made Laura shudder. Her heart raced, and still she rocked on.

But when the familiar rumble of a four-wheeler with no tail pipe broke into her thoughts, Laura planted her feet and leaned forward. The engine chugged oddly, nearly dying out before its unseen rider revved the gas and sped out toward the hollow. She turned to look for the deputy, but he wasn't beside the barn anymore.

Then the sheriff's SUV pulled up in front of the porch and he climbed out as Adam Richardson came heading toward them from the old garage. "Mornin', Sheriff."

"Morning. Everything quiet?" The sheriff opened his passenger side door and his Heinz 57 mix dog came bounding out to greet Laura.

Duke—a wolf hybrid combination of German shepherd, Alaskan malamute, and Siberian husky and who knew what else—would never be accepted in prominent breeding circles, but Laura was glad for his wild side. She and Blaine both owed their lives to the dog and his fearless instincts. Without hesitation, Duke had attacked the demon creature repeatedly to save them.

The deputy gestured toward the woods. "Well, sir, it was up until about a minute ago. Four-wheeler up that way, took off when he spotted me. But there's somethin' else you oughta see, back here." He gave a nod toward the garage. At the same instant, Duke alerted to a shift in the wind and took off ahead of them. Laura joined them, putting the back of her hand to her nose. A sickening smell now wafted toward her on the breeze as the group rounded the corner of the garage. Not ten feet from the far wall of the old shed lay a grisly heap of rotting bone and fur. Laura stepped around the men and stopped.

Loy's old hound, Rebel!

But it was impossible. The dog had died nearly a week before, killed by the very same beast they had fought off in the caves above Porter's Hollow. The same demon creature that had possessed her Uncle Curry till the end, and then disappeared with both Loy and Rebel's bodies.

Old Reb's belly was split from throat to tail and laid open, innards exposed. An overwhelming scent of whiskey clung to the poor creature, along with the pungent odor of animal musk. Its fur was soaking wet and matted with blood—and the eyes were missing. Laura cringed. Bile rose in her mouth and she turned away gagging.

Someone must have used Curry's moonshine to preserve the dog for just this moment.

"Jesus." Blaine put a hand on Laura's back.

She straightened and swallowed. Then, keeping her nose covered, forced herself to look once more. "What the..." she mumbled from behind her hand.

Deputy Richardson waved the air in front of his face. "Whew! Smells like somethin' raised a leg and marked the carcass."

Blaine inspected the remains. "Looks like it hasn't been here long. Grass isn't matted down or bloody." He looked around.

"You want me to head up into the woods a ways?" Adam asked. "See if I can find him?"

"Nah. You'd never catch up with Loy on foot anyway." Blaine pressed his lips together as he glared at the hound's remains.

"Yes sir," the deputy paused, staring hard at the carcass himself. "What the devil's got into that old fella?" He shook his head, his expression puzzled. "Why would Loy do such a thing to his own hound?"

Adam hadn't witnessed the creature Laura and Blaine had seen in the caves. He wasn't there that day, but Laura knew he'd heard about strange things going on in the hollow.

The young man frowned, then drew in a breath as his eyes widened. "Ya know," he turned to the sheriff, "if that *was* Loy out there on his old beat up ATV, he's gonna need gas for that thing from time to time. They still got an old farm tank out there at the Porter's."

The sheriff rubbed a hand across his buzz cut and replaced his cap. "Yeah, it'll be the one place he can't stay away from anyway, no matter what he's gotten himself into. I'll go by Beulah's later." Blaine studied the carcass a moment longer. Then to Adam he said, "You go on, get back to work. I've got things covered here."

Laura watched the deputy getting into his car. He glanced around, his expression reluctant. She wondered if he was looking for Cayley again. Then turning to the sheriff she said, "I'll get a shovel."

She disappeared into the garage for several minutes, returning with a large tarp as well.

"We're going to need to keep it, unfortunately." Blaine reached for the shovel and scooped the body up, laying it on the tarp, rolling the cover over it, and setting a rock on top. "I'll send somebody to pick it up." He wiped his brawny hands on his upper pant legs and the two of them walked back out the driveway. "Are you alright? You look a little pale."

"I'm fine." Laura surveyed the nearby woods. She thought of the old superstitious legend about the sound of an owl meaning death. Strangely enough, she'd heard one right here, before her father died. Then she'd heard another in the same tree on her second trip, before her mother died. She looked up at the shagbark hickory as they passed, half expecting to hear that same doleful hoot even now. Its branches quivered in the wind, but nothing more. *Owls don't appear in the daytime! Man, it was so easy to let this superstitious stuff get to you.*

Yet, as they climbed the porch steps a weighted silence descended.

Laura watched the trees on the far side of the field beyond the tobacco shed for several seconds, then she turned toward Blaine, wondering what he was thinking.

The sheriff spoke first. "I'm really sorry about your mother. I wish—" he cut himself off and shook his head. "Things don't get better by hashing them out over and over. How did it go with the funeral?"

"It was..." Tears threatened, but Laura squeezed them back and went on, "...a funeral she would have been proud of." She gave a soft wry laugh. "It was good, but I'll always feel like there were so many things we never got to say."

"Yeah, I know what you mean."

Laura sighed and lifted her chin to look up at him. They stood in silence, several seconds more, then he reached for her hand.

"I know it's not under the best of circumstances, but it's good to see you." His mouth curved into a soft smile, and he pushed her hair back from her face, brushing her skin.

"You too." Her stomach fluttered. She looked away and he sighed, letting his hand drop. The memory of his kiss the last time they'd seen each other caused the color to rise in her cheeks, but she wasn't ready for more just yet. She glanced at the house, biting her lip. "I should check on Aunt Hattie. She's napping." After a moment's pause she added, "She likes you, you know?"

"How's she doing?" Blaine asked as he opened the door, holding it for Laura to go ahead of him.

"Much better, but still not her old self yet." Laura excused herself to look in on her aunt. "Make yourself at home, I won't be long."

The woman was sleeping peacefully, but Laura couldn't resist pulling the blanket up over her further and pausing to watch her face. She finally closed the bedroom door and joined Blaine back downstairs where he sat in the living room on the chintz covered sofa. His broad shoulders rose above the back and his long legs stretched out in front. One hand hung loose over the end of the thickly stuffed couch arm. Laura's heart fluttered. *Get a grip. You've been eye to eye with the walking dead and faced off with a demon, for God's sake. He is just a man.* She cleared her throat.

Blaine turned at the sound and got up to meet her, taking her hands in his, standing there looking down at her like he expected... She drew a breath and turned away. "I've got coffee on and I can make you some breakfast."

He held onto one hand, turning her toward him again, tilting his head to one side. He watched her and waited. Then he pulled his hand away, tucking both into his pants pockets.

"I ate already. But I'll take you up on the coffee." He followed closely and stopped just inches behind Laura. He was so near she could feel his warmth and smell his cologne, but he only reached for the coffees when she turned.

Grateful she didn't have to test the steadiness of her hands, she sat down opposite him at the table. Her mind grasped for words. She longed to explain her misgivings about getting into a relationship with a man again so soon, but grappled with whether she should even try.

Her nervousness about her own sexuality was only part of the issue. She was beginning to enjoy her independence. No one to check with before she did things or made decisions, no one to answer to for how she spent her time or money, no one to have to adjust her life for while guessing his moods or reactions. And yet, she looked up at the man sitting across from her, and she got that breathless, light sensation in her stomach and something stirred in her groin despite her apprehension. "I'm sorry," she fumbled. "I'm just not used to... well... you know."

Blaine's eyebrows shot up. "What?" He grinned as she finally met his eyes. "Talking to a man?"

Laura laughed. "Not this way." She got serious again. "It's just, it's been a long time."

"Then let's make it easier on you. I'll just ask you out, and you can just say yes." He gave a soft laugh. Then he reached across the table and laid a large sun darkened hand over her smaller, paler one. Butterflies fluttered in her nether regions as his thumb caressed the soft underside of her wrist. "So, what do you say?"

"Hmm?" She'd been concentrating so intensely on his touch she nearly missed what he'd said. "Oh, what was it I'm supposed to say?" She smiled playfully, starting to pick up on the flirtatious mood. "Um, let me think. *Yes*. That was it."

He laughed again. Then added, "But only if you really want to."

Laura took a breath, staring into those soft green eyes. What was she afraid of, really? Old insecurities? New commitments? "I really do want to." She finally said, "In fact, I'd love to."

"This weekend. No more waiting for everything to be settled, or perfect. We get someone to stay with Hattie, and we'll go out on the town."

"Ooh, Grassy Creek? That might be a little racy for my blood."

"Oh, no, we can hit the big town. Go all the way to West Jefferson. You'd be surprised what you can get into there."

"Really?" It was her turn to raise an eyebrow.

"We can actually go out for a real sit-down dinner. Nice bottle of wine. If you like, we could even take in a movie at the Parkway. Or we could go all out and hit the VFW for burgers and fries, and maybe shoot some pool."

The smile playing at the corners of his mouth drew Laura in as he joked. "Hmm, surprise me," she said.

"Tell you what. Why don't we start out early? Maybe I can show you around the area, go for a hike? I can pick you up on Saturday, around one o'clock?"

"Sounds good, but I'll have to check with Cayley."

They'd been so wrapped up in conversation they didn't notice Hattie had come into the room till she opened the fridge.

"Oh, my, look at the time." Laura jumped up. "Aunt Hattie, can I get you anything?"

"No, no," the elderly woman brushed the wispy, white tendrils of hair out of her face. "I can manage. Just lookin' for a mid-mornin' snack. You two go on and visit. I'll be fine."

Blaine stood. "Actually, I need to be on my way. But you ladies enjoy your day. I'll check back with you later, make sure everything's okay."

Laura had assured Blaine she and her aunt would be fine without round the clock surveillance. Still, after sending Richardson off, he had called in to assign another deputy to stop by a few times.

At the door, Blaine leaned in close, keeping his voice low. "I'll visit Beulah Porter today. And I'll check back in with you this evening."

After the sheriff left, Laura thought she should have asked if she could go with him to Beulah's. But Hattie needed her attention. Time would come, and soon, to visit the other woman—preferably alone. She suspected her granny knew much more about the Porter family history than she'd been willing to reveal. Laura hoped to find a way to get Beulah to warm up to her only granddaughter.

CHAPTER 7

The Reverend Cecil Thomas Honeywell stepped out of his rental car in front of a rather small brick church in Normal, Illinois. This one was fronted by impressive twin towers at its corners, each topped with castle style parapets. Between them, the recessed façade of The Church of St. Joseph rose in a peak with a cross in the middle that reached the height of the tower tops. A narrow, arched slit directly below the cross harkened back to the days when even churches needed defense plans, while a large, round stained-glass *rose* window—or St. Catherine's window—graced the top center of the wall beneath the tiny arch.

The main entrance, set with heavy oak double doors and topped with a half-moon window called a lunette, jutted forward below this, meeting the tower walls at each side. To the left and right of the grandiose entrance were two more sets of smaller double doors. One most likely allowed direct, private access through to the confessional. The other probably served as an entrance to a side hall, with stairs leading down to the basement and up to the choir loft.

Tom had been in a wide variety of houses of worship over the years. He'd also studied church architecture, out of an amateur interest only, but it fascinated him. This one, like so many older Catholic churches, used an abundance of architectural styles and symbolism, despite its dwarfed size.

Tom grabbed the wrought iron handle and the thick door opened with a *whoosh*. The scent of candles, polished wood, and old carpet wafted over him like a heavy incense. When he'd called to let the parish priest, Father Gahlen Doherty, know he was getting close, the man had asked Tom to meet him here in the church nave. The door drifted shut and the room darkened for the

27

moment—the only light inside coming from the altar candles and the soft, beaming glow through the stained-glass windows. The atmosphere no doubt was meant to subdue and humble the vilest of sinners.

"Hello." A disembodied voice echoed around the room. "I'll be with you in a moment."

Still standing at the back of the nave, Tom twisted left and right, searching for the source. The same voice continued more quietly, "*In nomine Patris, et Filii, et Spiritus Sancti.*" Tom's eyes and ears finally located the priest, bowed before the altar at the foot of a large crucifix in the front center of the sanctuary. Father Gahlen crossed himself and stood. Placing a hand in the middle of his back, he stretched tall.

Tom made his way toward the front of the nave as the priest turned and descended the sanctuary steps. The man wore the traditional white clerical collar under a simple black cassock gathered at the waist by a red corded belt. A plain gold cross hung from his neck on a long gold chain. He was taller than Tom by several inches, broad through the chest, a wide imposing figure with a thick mustache and full beard.

Father Gahlen extended a large meaty hand. "Reverend Cecil Thomas Honeywell?" The deep baritone voice matched the size of the man as it resonated through the nave. Yet, from his gentle eyes and firm grip, calm assurance flowed like a spiritual presence.

"You can call me Tom, if you don't mind, Father."

The priest folded his hands in front of his robe. The two studied each other in silence a moment before the man spoke. "Father Gahlen Doherty, but then I suppose you guessed that."

Tom smiled and nodded. "I've been looking forward to meeting you." If he remembered correctly, Father Gahlen had to be nearly seventy, but he appeared much younger. Though his beard and hair were more salt than pepper, his eyebrows were mostly dark. And he had a youthful, roundish face despite the crinkles at his eyes and across his brow.

The big priest drew an audible breath. "Well, why don't we go over to the rectory? I'm sure you'll find it more comfortable there, and we can have a cup of coffee while we talk." He led the way through a side door onto a short walkway connecting the church to his personal quarters. "Maybe you can help me eat some of the cookies the kind-hearted ladies of this parish seem to think I need for sustenance." He patted his not insubstantial paunch with one hand as he opened the rectory door and stepped back for Tom to enter.

He followed Father Gahlen into his living room, where the priest motioned to one of two overstuffed recliners with a table between them. The well-worn look of the other one belied the priest's favorite spot. Tom took in the simple white walls. Large windows let in a flood of light, the wood floor was covered by several coordinating patterned rugs in tans and browns, and the rest of the furniture matched the recliners in soft cream tones. Spartan wooden end tables, like the one beside him, flanked the sofa.

Father Gahlen interrupted Tom's inspection of his surroundings. "Make yourself comfortable. How do you take your coffee?"

"Just black, please."

"Man after my own heart. Be right back."

Alone in the room, Tom noticed a set of bookshelves that piqued his curiosity. He rose to check out some of the titles. Many were typical clergy reading—expositions on scripture, various volumes of church history—but Tom was intrigued by the collection of works on architecture, classic literature, and art. The old priest's reading taste wasn't much different from his own. Yet, the limited number of books on exorcism drew Tom's attention enough to pull one of the few from the shelf. He studied the cover of the thin, slightly tattered paperback. *The Rite.* It was the story of a young American priest sent to Rome to study the topic under an old cleric there who routinely dealt with possession in his ministry.

"It's one of my favorites." The priest set a tray of coffee and cookies on the nearest end table. "Simple story. Ever read it?"

Tom shook his head. "No. Truth is, I never really wanted to deal with the whole idea of demons and possession." He sighed. "I mean, I studied it some in seminary. Then I decided it wasn't for me. Too—surreal—other worldly. I took Professor Lucas' class. He's the one who suggested I talk to you. I called him first, but he said his knowledge has only ever been academic."

Tom reached to put the book back, but the priest interrupted, "Take it with you. You can keep it, if you like, or mail it back. But it is one of the best books on exorcism I've ever read."

"Thank you." Tom lifted the book.

When they were seated, Father Gahlen helped himself to a bite of sugar cookie, appearing to savor it like a connoisseur before he spoke again. "So, you didn't come here to inspect my book collection. And from what you told me on the phone before, I don't suspect you're a dabbler wanting firsthand accounts of spinning heads, projectile vomiting, and levitating furniture? Otherwise, I wouldn't have agreed to see you."

The two ministers eyed each other in silence a moment before the big priest finally spoke again. "So, preacher, just exactly what is it you think you've seen?"

Tom washed his cookie down with a swig of coffee. Then he set the cup down and shifted in his chair toward the old priest. "I'm not sure where to begin. I have," he hesitated and started again, "well... I had an uncle who manifested something. Some other being, or entity. It took over his body, or at least it appeared to, but then it also became separate from him when he died."

Father Gahlen's mouth pressed shut, his brows drawn.

Tom continued, "It wasn't just another personality, Father. In fact, it wasn't even human."

The priest looked away, staring straight ahead for several seconds. He took a sip of coffee and set his mug down as well. "Okay, tell me about it. Can you describe this being? Did it speak? Did you try to talk to it? Did this just happen suddenly?"

Despite the guarded look the old priest eyed him with, the tension in Tom's jaw eased. He described the wolf-like creature he'd seen, and the way his Uncle Curry had morphed into it according to Laura's description. He'd seen the beast himself, but not the transformation that took place before her eyes. He told the old priest everything, pouring out his family's story before the cleric like a penitent at confession.

He described the rape and murder of Lottie Edwards, his father's claims of being tormented and manipulated by some evil being, how his Uncle Curry had involved him in hiding their sordid secret. He also told the priest about his great, great grandfather and his hoodoo practices and the old bowie knife that had been passed down through the family. And that now the creature appeared to be after his other uncle, Loy Porter.

Father Gahlen had been sitting forward on the edge of his seat while Tom talked. Now he slid back and sank down in his chair. Several seconds went by as the big priest stared off across the room, gripping the recliner. Then he dropped his head and closed his eyes, taking the gold cross on the chain around his neck in one huge paw.

Tom watched the other man's lips move silently for several minutes, uncomfortable, feeling compelled to join him in prayer, yet not wanting to disturb Father Gahlen's concentration. He found himself sweating, his hands tensed, clenching the chair arms.

At last, the old cleric crossed himself and looked up. His voice low and quiet now, he stared Tom in the eye. "These things you are talking about are not to be taken lightly or handled by a novice. Evil talismans and curses are the worst kind of signs." He sighed and asked, "What exactly is it you want from me?"

It took a few seconds before Tom could respond. "Help? Information? Advice." He sighed hard. "I was hoping you could tell me what to do. How to get rid of this thing, cast it out, send it back to hell, for God's sake!"

Father Gahlen got up and paced back and forth in the small space of open floor, fists clenched. "For God's sake? For God's sake?" He stopped and turned on Tom. "This is not something you can just assign the person a few hail Mary's for, or whatever your religious faith requires for penitence, and expect to go home and forget about it. What you've described to me is not just a matter of oppression, it's real, genuine possession. There's so much involved in handling these... these... beings. Nearly impossible to get rid of them. So much beyond you—and me." He finished dejectedly.

"So, it will be difficult, but surely not impossible?" Tom suggested.

The big priest's forehead was damp, and he'd gone a shade paler. "I haven't dealt with anything like this in years." He paced the room again as he talked. "I've been able to avoid it here in this quiet parish, thanks be to God!"

Once again, the old man stopped and turned to Tom. "You said the bodies were never found? But the eyes were taken and saved, by your uncle, not the creature?"

Tom eyed the man before he nodded in response. He wasn't sure it was possible, but Father Gahlen appeared to have gone even whiter.

"You don't understand." He stared down hard at Tom. "This is not a—a—small..." He cut himself off with a huff before he tried again. "It doesn't matter that this is some backwoods place no one would ever suspect of such a thing." The priest shook his head and grabbed the gold cross around his neck with a white-knuckled fist. "This creature may very likely have consumed the flesh of his victims and allowed your uncle to take his prizes to keep him enslaved. These things... these kind..." the priest appeared to search for words for several long seconds, "...these kinds of beings are pure evil, and once they've chosen a host—or a victim—it's dangerous business." The old cleric shook his head and repeated his earlier declaration, "Nearly *impossible* to cast them out."

The Baptist minister remained silent, watching the Catholic priest's face, waiting, hoping Father Gahlen would argue himself into the conclusion Tom sought.

"And you? You know nothing about it. You don't know what you're getting yourself into, man."

Tom rose from his chair. Drawing himself up to full height, he finally suggested what he'd really come for. "That's why I need you to come to Porter's Hollow and help me."

The big priest shrank away, literally. Appearing to deflate as he blew the words out in one breath, "No, no. Absolutely not. I'm sorry, young man." Then he shook his head vehemently and declared, "I'm afraid that *is* impossible."

CHAPTER 8

October 1968

Laurie wasn't sure how long she lay there in that dank cellar afraid to move, afraid to make a sound, but she finally realized it could be a lot longer before anyone found her down there. It hadn't been used since Granny Beulah quit gardening, 'cause her eyesight was going bad. She'd have to do something.

But she was sure if she moved, something would jump out of the dark and snatch her away forever.

She didn't know how long she sat there, curled up in fear, trying to summon her courage, but suddenly something warm and fuzzy began to crawl up her leg. She tried so hard to be still. Not let it know she was a living thing. But just as it reached her thigh, and she thought she could stand it no longer, the cellar door slammed open and in the sudden intense white light she saw the big black spider on her leg. And beyond that, through the bright glare, a dark figure descended.

Her bladder let loose and she screamed. And then she moved. She moved so quick even the spider didn't have time to react. Tearing past the hands extended to grab her, eight-year-old Laurie Porter ran for her life.

CHAPTER 9

Wednesday, November 17, 2010

The knock on the door startled Laura out of deep preoccupation. Aunt Hattie was safely tucked in bed, and Laura had been doing an internet search on demons in history. She'd called Tom earlier to talk. His wife, Elizabeth, said he was out of town but she expected him back in the morning. She promised she'd tell him to call Laura as soon as possible.

Oh well, soon enough. Though she'd been anxious to find out the creature's secrets, there was a part of her that had begun to resist facing this thing—like some new element had crept in causing her to hesitate. Something in the suffocating sensation, and the other young girl's expression from her vision, gave her pause.

The knocking grew louder, more insistent.

Laura stepped to the right side of the entrance, away from the window. "Who is it?"

"Blaine."

She had left the porch light on, expecting the sheriff. Still she lifted the curtain and peeked before unlocking the door.

"You okay?" He peered hard at her. Duke wiggled around the man and made his way in to sit at her side.

"Yeah. Just being cautious." Shutting the door, she waved him and the dog in to the kitchen. "I was a little preoccupied." Snapping the laptop shut, Laura pushed it aside along with the book, and reached for the wine bottle and her almost empty glass to clear them away. A self-conscious blush warmed her cheeks.

Blaine had other ideas. "I wouldn't mind a glass of that, if you're sharing?"

She raised her eyebrows at him with a smile.

"I'm off duty."

Producing the other large globe glass, she half-filled them both and sat down across from Blaine with Duke at her side, his head on her leg, blinking up at her. A warm sensation, not entirely wine induced, coursed through Laura. This was homey, cozy— almost too much so. A gentle smile graced her mouth as she rubbed the dog's head.

Blaine's voice flowed into her thoughts, fitting into her mind like one she'd known all her life. "I went to visit Beulah today. Had to wake her up from a nap." He gave a soft laugh and shook his head. "Your grandmother's a tough old bird, rough exterior, but she's got a tender heart when it comes to her boys. Claims she hasn't seen or heard from Loy since he disappeared two weeks ago, but I'm not so sure. There were signs—fresh smell of gas, wood cut and stacked—things she couldn't do."

Laura bit her lip in thought before she answered. "She does love them—fiercely. I've been wondering if she doesn't just choose to ignore what they've done, just to protect her own world. To keep from having to face the past. It's hard to admit you might be partly responsible for allowing something like that to go on under your nose." Laura frowned at that last thought—it resonated with her, bringing up the accusing image of the young woman's face from her latest visions, and her lungs tightened.

Blaine got her attention again. "You suggesting she's known what her sons have been involved in all these years, and said nothing?"

She let out a breath. "I'm not saying... I mean I don't know, but they were all she had, and now she probably believes she's lost them forever, because of us. Or rather because of me."

He sighed deep. "Damn. I sure as hell don't want to have to bring a woman in her mid-nineties down to the precinct to be questioned."

"Don't." She looked him in the eye. "Let me talk to her. I'm her only granddaughter. Maybe she'll tell me more if I can spend some time with her. Maybe I can get her to understand there's still time to find Loy and save him from..." she shook her head in frustration, "...from whatever's going on."

Blaine pressed his mouth in a tight line for the moment, appearing to think over her suggestion. Then his features relaxed and he nodded. "Okay, but you need to let me know what happens."

He focused his gaze on the laptop and book she'd shoved aside and took a sip of his wine. Then he stood abruptly and held out a hand to her. "I've got an idea."

Laura lifted her chin in response, realizing how much she liked the hard line of his jaw, especially with the few days' beard growth and mustache he sported. She liked the way his green eyes sparkled, and his forehead lifted when his mood lightened. She also liked the way he reached for her hand and helped her to her feet.

"You got any good movies on DVD? Something light and entertaining? Let's both relax a little. This stuff gets pretty intense, especially if you're not used to investigating things like murder for a living." He laughed but she knew he meant it for her.

She had to admit, the visions were becoming more frequent and more intense. She could use a distraction, and a little human connection—and it certainly didn't hurt that it was with a man who gave her butterflies.

Laura reached for a box she'd left on the floor by the television. "I brought a few of my own movies along, but I'm not sure I have anything you'll like."

"You pick one."

She browsed the titles a moment, then with an 'aha' sort of smile, she pulled out *Bounty Hunter* and held it up. "It's a chick-flick."

He gave a mock bow of submission and waved a hand toward the TV before settling into one corner of the sofa, stretching out his long legs.

She raised a shoulder, tilting her head. "It's light, funny, and romantic. About as far from the murderous, psychic, and paranormal as possible."

Blaine patted the sofa next to him and Laura felt the color rise in her face again. Still she sat beside him, taking a few seconds to get situated, and finally relaxed against him. Duke snuggled down at their feet as the movie started, while Blaine draped an arm over her shoulders. They ended up talking through most of the movie anyway, but she didn't mind.

He'd gotten married young, at eighteen, and left for the Army within a year. The two were the same age, high-school sweethearts, and he'd meant it to last forever. But when he came home on leave and told her he intended to re-enlist, she'd gone off the deep end.

"Said she couldn't take the tension, worrying if I'd be killed, or injured so bad I wouldn't know her anymore." Blaine stared off across the room. "She was fine with it all when I first joined up. But she seemed different when I came back. Like something had her spooked. Said she had a weird feeling about things. That something bad was going to happen and I shouldn't leave her."

Laura laid a hand on his leg. Watching his face, she could see the pain and confusion in his expression even now.

"I tried to calm her down, reassure her, but..." Blaine rubbed his face. "I only had two weeks leave." He paused again and shook his head. "The morning I had to go, she told me she wasn't sure she'd be there when I got back. I tried to reason with her, but she just clammed up. I tried calling. Sent letters. She never answered. Even tried sending a friend out to check the place. But she wasn't there, and when I got back, she was still gone."

Laura couldn't understand. *Who would do that to a man going off to the Army? Why wouldn't she at least write?* She tried to be careful what she said to Blaine. She didn't want to open old wounds. "You mean you've never heard from her since? No divorce papers, nothing?"

The muscles in his jaw flexed and he turned to face her. "No. Nothing." He was quiet for several seconds before he went on, "I talked to the manager at the 7-Eleven where she worked at the time. He said one day Lilly just didn't come in. They tried to call her, but she never answered. And it wasn't like her to do that."

"Did she have any other family?" Laura asked.

"She had a much older step-sister, but I had no idea how to get in touch with her. Never even met her, and they didn't communicate. I suppose there's some chance I could locate Lilly through missing persons. But I've just never had the heart for it, not yet anyway. I just wanted to forget." He studied Laura's face and drew a breath before he added, "So, if that's a problem, I'll understand."

Laura bit her lip as she thought. At last she said, "No, I guess not. I mean... let's just take this one step at a time. Right?"

He nodded and went back to watching the movie, or at least pretended to. Laura wasn't sure, but they were both quiet for some time, until something in the movie made them both laugh and the tension began to ease.

When Blaine left later—much later—Laura found, once again, she couldn't sleep. She could feel his beard scratching her face, his lips on hers where he'd kissed her—just once—before he left. His warmth still lingered on her body where he'd held her against him.

Yet, now her mind raced all over the place. Was she getting in too deep, too soon with him? He wasn't even really divorced. And it might confuse and cloud the professional side of their relationship. He was the sheriff and she was a woman whose family was connected to the deaths of... who knew how many innocent women. And the real murderer was still out there, possibly hunting them both for their part in Curry's death.

The creature had lost its long-term host because of them, and now its only consort was Loy, mentally disabled from birth, and without a mean bone in his body. Could it turn him?

Could the demon change him into something as evil as his brother Curry?

CHAPTER 10

Thursday, November 18, 2010

Several boxes still sat unpacked in Laura's room, mostly books she needed to get new shelves for. But one held a hunting knife with a leather sheaf she could slip over her belt. She grabbed it, her digital camera, and her hiking stick and headed downstairs where she stopped to check on Aunt Hattie—again.

Looking from the elderly woman to Cayley, Laura said, "You sure you two don't mind me going out for awhile?" Then she leaned in and kissed Aunt Hattie on the cheek.

The elderly woman patted Laura's arm. "You just be careful. You ain't lived around here in some time. Don't you go gettin' yourself lost now, ya here?"

Cayley smiled. "You go on and get some fresh air. We'll be just fine."

Laura guessed the young woman to be in her twenties. A robust, healthy country girl. Not heavy, but not pencil thin either. She was taller than Laura by a few inches, but that wasn't saying a lot. She guessed Cayley to be about 5' 4", and athletic. The girl's well-defined leg muscles were evident in the hospital scrubs she wore every day. Maybe a runner or a climber? A woman who inspired confidence and trust in more ways than one.

Laura smiled back. "I'll have my cell, and I won't be more than an hour or so." Heading out the back hall, she noticed the old twelve-gauge shotgun leaning against the pantry wall. She thought about grabbing it too, but she didn't want to take the only weapon in the house and leave the other women without. Aunt Hattie still didn't know about Loy, but Laura had given the CNA a brief explanation—leaving out the actual demon creature, of course.

She'd told Cayley that Loy had survived a rather violent scuffle with his brother Curry and run off. Laura claimed that he'd been upset, and no one could predict how he would act if found, but she didn't want to alarm her aunt with the news. She'd told the girl to keep her eyes and ears open, but it wasn't likely he'd come around too close since he was trying to avoid being questioned.

Cayley had simply nodded and told Laura, "Don't you worry. I won't let any harm come to Hattie."

Laura had been impressed once again by the girl's demeanor, but she felt guilty about the white lies, especially since Cayley was a friend of Tom's, and Laura truly hoped they would eventually find their own sort of friendship beyond the professional need of help for her aunt. Still, you couldn't just go telling people there's a demon prowling around the county like it was a stray dog they needed to watch out for. Especially the Certified Nursing Assistant caring for your elderly aunt. She might decide you were the one in need of special care—in a mental ward. Most people wouldn't believe you anyway.

The back screen door slapped shut behind Laura, as she stepped out onto the path into the woods behind Aunt Hattie's leading into Porter's Hollow. The mid-morning sun shone down, but was subdued by a cool wind and a growing cloud bank to the south, it didn't provide much warmth.

Setting out on a carpet of red and yellow leaves spotted brown with late fall rot, Laura buttoned her flannel shirt and zipped her quilted vest against the chill. She looked up at the tall, thin, mostly bare oak trees swaying wildly above, and surveyed the white pines shuddering with every gust. A red squirrel sat on a moss-covered boulder, nibbling an acorn, but it scurried away when it spotted her, and a raven perched on a bare limb overhead, squawking out a scolding, *rawk, rawk,* before taking off.

The world around her appeared peaceful and calm as she settled into a strong but comfortable rhythm, her hiking stick thumping the ground every fourth step. Laura lifted her head and took a deep breath, enjoying the damp piney scent of the forest.

In little more than a quarter of an hour she came to Porter's Hollow Road where she made a left, then dog-legged right onto Porter's Creek Road. She could see the rooftop of Granny Beulah's house well below to her right. This road would take her up to the rugged trail that went back through the woods to the old Hadley cabin, the same trail she'd partly cleared the last time she was here. To be honest, she hadn't set out with a plan to go back there, but now that she thought about it, there might be some chance she'd find evidence of Loy's whereabouts. It was possible he'd use the old place to stay in sometimes, the way Curry had. And though she was certain the sheriff would have checked it out, still she felt drawn to the place.

The trail came into view and Laura slowed her pace. The back of her neck prickled with a creeping sensation. She stopped to survey the road in both directions, scanning the woods before stepping onto the wild mountain trail. The sun still peeked through the canopy covering the road and the mountain to both sides. The only sounds were the occasional bird chatter and the constant sighing wind. Still she couldn't shake her growing uneasiness.

She continued up the trail, glancing around, eyes and ears sharp, but nothing more than the leaves and a few small animals stirred. By the time she reached the Hadley cabin, where she'd been attacked by her Uncle Curry a few weeks before, she'd worked up a sweat.

At the bottom of the porch steps she paused, studying the place, listening, shivering... as much from an uneasy sense of foreboding as from the cool breeze ruffling her damp clothing. The two combined to leave her teeth chattering for the moment. She reached back and pulled the hunting knife out of its sheaf at her hip before she stepped forward once again. The sun managed to shine a beam of light directly onto the tightly closed front door. The last time she'd been here it had been left ajar by Curry, who'd shoved it open to give her chase.

She took another hesitating step and waited again, then continued up to the landing where she checked in the windows and listened. When all remained quiet, she finally shoved the door as far open as she could all at once and jumped back.

The wood scraped and creaked as dust puffed up to float on the sunbeams. Laura waited for the air to clear before venturing inside. A single mug with a spoon in it, a sugar bowl, and a jar of instant coffee sat on the table in the main room. She made her way to the adjoining single bedroom where she discovered an old mattress, along with a blanket and pillow, pushed up into one corner. Making her way back out into the main room, she checked the cupboards and found a few cans of food and some paper plates. The sink had been rinsed clean, a bucket of water sitting beside it—and taped to the counter top was a piece of paper bearing her name in Loy's now familiar scrawl.

Mis Larie,
Ples don com heer no mor
i will not let the beest git you
i will tak kar of you
i will git rid of it if it meens dyin'
but you kin not com <u>heer</u>
ever agin

A rush of breath escaped Laura and she backed away from the counter, that creeping feeling of being watched sending goosebumps spreading up her arms. She felt, as much as saw in her peripheral vision, the shadow that entered the room. Spinning on one heel to find Loy standing in the doorway, she froze. He was bigger than the Loy she knew, and he stood with feet spread, one hand working vigorously at opening and then closing into a tight fist, the other wrapped around the handle of the old bowie knife. Before she could speak, the man's cold, placid face changed, contorting with emotion. His eyes were full of pain, fear, sorrow.

In an instant, she took in his bulk, his torn and dirty clothing, his scratched and bloodied face, arms and hands, just before he stumbled over the threshold and staggered into the room.

Stung into action by a flood of adrenaline, Laura gripped her own knife, inching to the right, not brandishing the weapon, but adjusting her hold on it firmly. Loy stumbled further into the room, moving toward the table that now lay between them. His face twisted first into a painful grimace, then into an evil sneer and back, and with the changes he became two different beings, like the transformation of Jekyll and Hyde.

He appeared to trip over his own feet. Dropping forward, he slapped his free hand on the table, and with his head hanging down, he began to growl, low and deep, still in a man's voice but with an animal-like sound. Then his head came up and the hand clutching the knife flipped it like a baton twirler, so fast Laura couldn't trace its motion. All at once he reared back and pointed the blade downward, arm raised above his head. The growl deepened. Increasing in volume, it became more animal and less human as it grew. His eyes turned yellow and the bones of his face appeared to rearrange themselves.

Then the noise erupted into an unearthly scream, piercing the air and echoing around the cabin walls as the knife hand came down, jabbing the blade into the tabletop with a *thwack*. And the visceral shriek ended in a very human agonized groan.

Laura had kept inching her way around the table toward the door, realizing she had no hope of getting through to her uncle in this condition. Now she jumped and screamed, but she hesitated only a second before dashing for the door. She took the porch steps in a single leap and landed hard on a protruding rock, twisting her left ankle. Searing pain shot up her leg, but she kept moving.

Run-hopping fast, Laura headed for the trail down the mountain, but she stumbled and fell, one knee scraping rock. The sudden sharp pain dropped her onto her rear end in the dirt. And all went quiet. Holding her breath, she looked back at the cabin door and listened.

The large form filled the doorway again, and Laura scrambled to her feet. Pain shot up her leg from her ankle as she tore through the brambles. Her other knee had taken the whole force of her weight when she went down. Now it burned as it bled through her pant leg. Branches swatted her face though she used her arms to shield herself. Keeping her legs moving, she chanced a quick look. The creature was gaining on her fast as she struggled to ignore the pain.

Then suddenly the air split like a lightning crack with a sound that pierced her very soul. The haunting, agonized scream erupting mere feet behind her both startled Laura to a stop and tore at her heart. She glanced back to see her Uncle Loy double over and drop to his knees. He held the knife poised over his left wrist and rocked.

His body deflated, she could think of no other way to describe it, and he whimpered like a whipped pup. Despite her own fear and pain, she didn't run now.

"S-s-s-s-s-Sorry. S-s-s-So. S-s-s-Sorryyyyy," he cried. "D-d-d-didn' wanna..." he pressed the knife into his wrist, drawing blood. "Gotta protec..."

Laura hobbled toward the broken figure, heart wrenching at the anguished tone in his voice. "Don't do that," she pleaded. Cringing, she stepped closer as Loy continued to draw the blade across his skin. Fresh wounds patterned both wrists and arms from where he'd punished himself. "You don't have to do that." She quickened her steps and reached for him, putting her hand out to stay his. Gentle but firm, she grasped his bony forearm.

He looked up then, tears streaming down his dirty face, eyes pleading. He shook his head. "H-haf ta c-cut... th-the devil... bleed 'im out."

"No, please, let me help you." Aware of the precariousness of her situation, Laura pressed on anyway. "*No one* wants to hurt you. Tom and I want to help. In fact, he's talking to someone right now who knows about this kind of thing." She thought the mention of the preacher might give Loy hope, but his face registered no change. Then she added, "The sheriff doesn't want to hurt you either."

Loy's face went still. His features hardened, and in a perfectly clear, deep voice, heavy with lewd suggestion he canted, "Oooh, the big handsome sheriff wants to help, does he? Help who?" His head came up and he stared hard into Laura's eyes. Not missing a single word or letter, in a voice not his own he sneered, "Help you, bitch? Yeah, I'll bet he does, but I can help you like that." Lips curling, he tilted his head at an odd angle, looking at her from the corners of his eyes. "Just like I helped..." He halted, leering at her, licking his lips like he had a delicious secret he savored at her expense. He growled then, a sensual snarling growl.

Laura had dropped her grip on his arm and backed away when he started to speak. Now she bumped into a tree behind her, and though every nerve in her body screamed, "Run," she couldn't move. His eyes seared into her, burning away her defenses so that her very soul was exposed, leaving her vulnerable to the vile, evil thoughts and images in his mind. The scene that played out there rattled Laura while the creature's words confused her, held her captive, froze her limbs and squeezed her chest with their cold intent. The air had turned foul, and she found it hard to breathe, and despite every instinct warning her against it, she couldn't tear her eyes away from his. He stood then, rising up off the ground in one lithe movement, right hand raising the knife.

Just when Laura thought he would lunge for her, Loy's eyes— not the beast's—met her own. For several long seconds his face twisted in agonized silence, tears leaving dirty streaks on his face again. His swelling body tensed, and his knife arm trembled, lowering as if he had to force it down. But finally, it dropped to hang limp at his side and his whole being sagged. Then without another sound, he turned and fled.

CHAPTER 11

Slipping through the back door, Laura peeked around the corner. Aunt Hattie was busy in the kitchen with her back toward the hall and Cayley was nowhere in sight. Laura made her way across the sitting room, breathless and still trembling, to creep up the stairs, unseen. She'd barely got the bathroom door closed when she heard footsteps.

"That you, Miss Laura?" the CNA called out.

"Yeah, I'm back. I'll be down in a few minutes. Just want to clean up and change." Forcing calmness into her voice, she waited, hoping the younger woman hadn't seen her.

"Okay, no problem. Hattie and I were just about to have lunch. We'll set you a place, too."

Laura stopped to study herself in the mirror—hair askew, jeans torn, blood trailing down her pant leg, a sight that most definitely would have raised questions. Grunting as she peeled them off, she threw the jeans away and cleaned up. Now with fresh clothes and well bandaged wounds, and a little makeup, she didn't appear too much the worse for wear. Though she'd walk with a slight limp for a few days, she'd simply tell people the truth. She'd slipped and turned her ankle hiking.

But looking into her own deep hazel-green eyes she imagined she saw something wild, something frightened, or maybe *frightful*. Something she had never seen there before. She'd been exposed to horrible depths of evil in the creature's gaze. She'd seen the girl from her vision in its eyes, writhing in pain, gasping for breath, and then it was her own lungs constricting. The girl and the creature's accusing gazes bore into her, insinuating her guilt. She could have saved them all since Lottie, every last one of them, but she had been afraid. She'd always been afraid. Laura turned away from her own image appalled.

Cayley called out, "Lunch is on the table."

Laura brushed her hair, attempting to reduce the wild look, but when she sat down to eat, Cayley stared at her openly. Laura avoided the girl's eyes and began eating.

A few seconds later the redheaded CNA said, "You take a spill out there somewhere?"

Laura knew her face reddened but she kept her voice calm. "It's embarrassing. I mean I hike all the time, but yeah, I stumbled over hidden tree roots and took a tumble down the hill."

To change the subject quickly Laura asked Cayley, "What do you like to do in your spare time? You do any hiking?"

"Oh, sure. I love it. Used to do it all the time when I was a kid. I was an only child and my dad taught me all the stuff he would've taught a boy. Hiking, boating, fishing, shooting, hunting even. Used to go by myself all the time when I was younger." She bit her lip, and studied her plate again. Then for reasons Laura found curious, Cayley shook her head as if at her own thoughts and said, "Just haven't really felt much like it since I came back."

The girl went back to eating without looking at Laura and the conversation moved on to Hattie's mouth-watering apple pie awaiting them.

Later in the afternoon out of sheer exhaustion, Laura drifted off while trying to read. Disturbing dream images of the young woman writhing under the weight of the demon-wolf assailed her. But this time the vision changed faces and shapes, hair color, eyes, age, taking so many identities Laura lost count. Moving faster and more contorted as they changed, they invaded the strange shrouded domain that often held her captive just between consciousness and REM sleep.

"Tom? Sorry, I mean Reverend. Come on in." Cayley's voice rose above the dream din. Then more loudly, Laura heard Cayley offer, "I can wake her for you."

Laura stirred. Throwing off the blanket and sitting up, she swept her hair back from her face. Her pulse quick, breath shallow, she tried to shake off the lingering veil of horror.

"No, no. I'll just leave a note..." Tom spoke in a softened but audible voice.

Catching her half-brother in mid-sentence, Laura called out, "I'm awake."

As he materialized in front of her sleep-fogged eyes, his long, tall shadow fell over her and she shivered. "Hey, sleepyhead. How's it going?"

"Um, fine. I was just trying to read up on things and drifted off." She stood and made a fuss of folding the blanket to give herself time to calm her senses. "Went hiking this morning. Must have been all the fresh air."

Tom tilted his head and raised his eyebrows but didn't say anything.

"Let's get some coffee," she suggested.

Laura made her way to the kitchen with Tom following. His presence helped settle her senses, his strong, deep baritone voice reassuring. "Sorry I couldn't get back to you yesterday. Elizabeth said you called. But I was visiting that priest I told you about." He glanced over his shoulder.

Laura poured a cup for each of them and leaned back against the counter taking a deep swig of black coffee. "She doesn't know," Laura replied.

"Cayley, or Hattie?" Tom had recommended the CNA from his church, but Laura didn't realize they were on first-name terms. One day she'd fit in around here—eventually. If only she and her mother had never left. Maybe all of this would have been settled long ago, and Laura wouldn't feel like a stranger in her own hometown.

To her brother she simply said, "Well, neither one, really. Of course, Aunt Hattie knows about most of it, but she doesn't know Loy is alive, or what happened to him. And Cayley doesn't really know anything, except that Loy is alive and we aren't telling Aunt Hattie for now."

"Hmm, well, we may have to let Cayley in on the situation at some point. Wouldn't be good to have her taken by surprise if something should happen here while everyone else is gone." He rubbed his beard stubble and drew an audible breath. "She was born and raised in this area. I doubt anything we tell her will be much of a surprise. I'm sure she's heard the old stories, as well as the recent rumors."

Laura observed him for a moment, wondering what connection he might have had with the girl in the past, overwhelmed with how little she herself knew about him. "Hmm, maybe that would best be left to you then," she commented, still watching his face. "Don't want her thinking I'm too crazy to take care of my elderly aunt."

They sat down at the kitchen table and Laura decided she should tell him about her newest visions. They'd come to Laura every night since she'd been back here, and now she'd seen other young girls in the creature's eyes somehow. And always with a view from the mountain overlooking her Granny Beulah's house. Though she couldn't put into words how it made her feel, the visions played like a movie in her mind, so clear Laura was sure the events were real. Something the demon-wolf wanted her to see, at least to inspire the fear that she was guilty by association as a Porter. Yet, she couldn't help but sense it knew something she didn't, and it savored the knowledge.

"You believe this is another victim reaching out to you?" He appeared to contemplate the idea. "I don't know. But then, I wouldn't have believed this beast was real a few months ago either. All the same, I don't think it's a good idea for you to try to communicate with something like that. It's dark stuff, consorting with the spirits of the dead. It could open you up to the creature's influence."

Deciding better not to argue the point, Laura told him about Loy coming at her with the four-wheeler on the farm lane. Of course, she said nothing about this morning's run-in. She didn't want Tom to tell Blaine. Both would consider it a direct threat. She didn't want them to give up on Loy's innocence... not when he so desperately wanted to fight the thing off.

When she finished speaking, Tom pulled out a small paperback book and laid it on the table. On the cover was a close-up of a priest's robe with two male hands cradling a beaded rosary.

"That's the only helpful thing I came away with from my trip to Normal."

Laura raised an eyebrow.

"Illinois, that is."

She reached for the book, turning it over to read the back cover.

"I asked him to come himself to see what he could do to help, but..." Tom shrugged as she glanced up, then added, "His advice was limited, other than to read that book."

She finished perusing the paperback, and laying it down, gave him the same raised eyebrow again.

Tom said, "It's as simple as it is arcane—near impossible for the most devout—yet an ordinary man can do it."

"I'm sorry? I don't follow you."

"Casting out demons." Tom gestured with both hands as if tossing something into the air. "Exorcism," stopping to point at the book he finished, "that's pretty much what it says."

Eyes wide, Laura stared at him several seconds. "Surely you don't propose we attempt to perform an exorcism on Loy—by ourselves?"

Again, Tom gave a shrug. "Father Gahlen flat out refused to come help. That was it, no explanation. But I believe it can still be done. More importantly, I think it's what *has* to be done in this case, not just for Loy but for the whole hollow, and..." he hesitated, dropping his gaze with a guilty look, "...for our family in particular. This thing will keep looking for us and our descendants. It will torment and beleaguer the women, and it will oppress and possess the men for as long as even one Porter lives and breathes. And it has all the time in the world. It's not limited to any one generation. I think it may prefer this area, but I know it has chosen this family."

Laura gaped at him. "We don't know that for sure," she insisted.

"It found you, didn't it? Got you back here, *and* your momma. And look what happened."

"That was our father's doing. *He* called me, not the creature."

Tom stared her in the eye. "And he was influenced by the demon. He said as much himself." Tom leaned forward, both elbows on the table. "Look, there's a combination of ways these things get at people. Oppression can be almost as bad as literal possession. Our daddy lived in hiding, suffering under the weight of what he'd done, kept there by that thing. Not a direct vessel for it but controlled by it nonetheless. Curry let it in. He was possessed, even though it apparently came and went, letting him live his life to some degree. We don't know for sure what it's doing to Loy yet. I suspect it's trying to do the same to him, and with his mental limitations—who knows what will happen."

"I know, but... us? Performing an exorcism?" *This is crazy. He can't be serious...* "How do you plan to get him to go along with it? And do you even know how?"

Tom sat back in his chair and rubbed a hand over his jaw. "I haven't figured it all out yet. But it's basically just praying over the person—for a long time—telling the demon to leave, using scriptures. Keeping at it till it works." He cocked his head in thought, eyes raised. "Might need to get some holy water. Catholics believe strongly in using it in real, or what they call solemn exorcisms. Oh, and crosses. The hard part is finding Loy or getting him to come to us. And we may have to tie him down unless we can get enough help to hold him."

The memory of Loy cutting his own wrists juxtaposed with the evil leering look and unnatural voice coming from him made Laura shudder, but she only said, "I think we'd need a lot more help to face down that thing."

"Like I said, I'm going to contact Father Gahlen again. Hopefully he's had time to consider our desperation and offer more. In the meantime, I'll get things together. I've found a few Catholic prayers of exorcism, though they're only supposed to be said by a priest. And I've read and reread the passages about the ones Christ performed." Tom sighed, deep, before continuing, "We've got to do something. We can't just leave Loy to fight this thing by himself, and we can't let it continue to roam the hollow, raping and murdering women."

Bottom lip clenched between her teeth, Laura avoided Tom's eyes. He was right. They couldn't let this go on. She knew she ought to tell him about what happened earlier, but she needed time to think things through. Maybe, just maybe, if they caught Loy at the right moment, he'd be willing to go along with their idea.

Tom's voice cut into her thoughts. "You know it's only a week till Thanksgiving. It would be better to take care of this situation before then, rather than have it hanging over the celebration."

She drew a heavy breath. "I guess it would. Are you and your family still coming?"

"We'll be here, early. Elizabeth wants to help with the prep. The kids and grandkids will come along later. What about your daughter. Is she still coming?"

Laura nodded through the fear and worry twisting a knot in her stomach. If they didn't have things settled by then, Tara might be in danger as well.

As if he read her mind, Tom said, "We can do this, little sister. We'll get this thing out of Porter's Hollow before it can hurt anyone else." He tilted his head to meet her eye. "You know it's not *how much* faith we have, but who we put our faith in. Mine is rooted in a higher power and I don't intend to wait around any longer to try and build more. Baptists believe we're all saints in Christ, and we all have the authority to command evil, if we just have faith."

Shaking her head to clear her mind of the images of Loy fighting the demon for control, Laura met Tom's gaze. "I hope you're right."

He stood and stretched his back. "I'll be in touch with Father Gahlen tomorrow. But it would be nice to have Sheriff Wilson on our side. I'll talk to him about it. Loy hasn't really done anything illegal—not as far as we know." He looked down at her. "Even so, I suspect it's going to be difficult to get the sheriff to go along with the idea. I'm sure he'll need some convincing." He winked at Laura. "You might have to help with that." He grinned despite the gravity of the situation.

Laura's cheeks burned, but she only made a face at her brother. Walking to the door with him, she said, "We'll be going shopping tomorrow for Thanksgiving. Tell Elizabeth to call me if she wants to go along. We can pick her up on our way out."

"Will do." Tom waved with the small book on exorcism clutched in his hand, then climbed into his truck.

Laura shivered at the unintended, but ominous symbolism.

CHAPTER 12

Friday, November 19, 2010

Wrestling under the weight of his studies, Tom leaned back in his desk chair. Elizabeth was out shopping with Laura, Aunt Hattie, and the Certified Nursing Assistant he'd recommended—Cayley O'Donnell—another issue that still burdened his conscience. One he'd never mentioned to his wife. He told himself it was for Cayley's sake. She was young and didn't deserve to live under the stain of past indiscretions.

As for how he could excuse himself, he'd only been ministering at the Ashe County Baptist Church a few weeks when he met the vivacious redhead. A middle-aged man struggling with his own identity, he'd been woefully unprepared and ill-equipped to deal with the troubled young beauty who came to him for advice. Tom sighed and shook his head at himself. He'd handle the whole situation differently if she came to him today.

Tom spent eight years in seminary earning his doctorate in pastoral studies, lingering longer than most at the effort intentionally. Then he'd only been an assistant pastor at several churches in various places, filled mostly with mature to elderly parishioners, before answering the call to come back to North Carolina to take on a pastorate of his own. A dark past had long overshadowed his desire to administer to an entire congregation. After all, he'd let a murderer, and a demon, continue to plague Porter's Hollow all those years. When forced to assist his father, or turn him in, he'd eventually run... drifting from town to town and job to job till he ended up meeting Elizabeth at a little church in Maryland.

Sitting at home alone in his study now, Tom struggled to get his thoughts back on the issue at hand. The process of exorcism could be read about, even envisioned, but actually performing such a rite... his insides churned, and his palms warmed. He let out a long slow breath, staring at the phone. Then reaching for the handset before he had time to change his mind, he dialed Father Gahlen's number.

"Hello," the old priest's booming voice greeted Tom cheerfully.

"Hello, Father. This is Tom, Tom Honeywell." He paused to allow the man time to recall their meeting before prompting, "You remember me?"

The growing silence on the other end of the line indicated the big cleric recalled, but maybe preferred otherwise. Finally, he said, "Yes, Reverend Honeywell, I remember you." He sighed into the phone.

Tom imagined the man crossing himself, perhaps turning pale and sweating.

"So, what can I do for you?" Father Gahlen at least attempted polite discourse.

Tom decided to approach the topic from a practical, student seeking advice vantage. "You know that situation we discussed? Well, I've read the book you gave me, and I've found more material with prayers and processes used by other clerics. Mostly of the Catholic church."

He waited for some response, but Father Gahlen remained silent.

"I'd like to ask your opinion on the ones I think sound most..." Tom searched for a word that wouldn't commit the priest to direct instruction in exorcism, "...meaningful."

Another sigh. "Go ahead."

"Well, for instance, one prayer, the one I like most begins, *Prayer to St. Michael the Archangel in the name of the Father, and of the Son, and of the Holy Ghost.* It goes on to invoke the archangel to defend those petitioning God in the battle against powers and principalities, and rulers of this dark world, and spirits of wickedness in high places. You know, just like it says in the scripture in Ephesians."

"I'm familiar with the invocation."

"Okay. Then you know it goes on with a long petition to Michael asking him to invoke God's help for us. Then it comes to the really long part where the petitioner prays for the power of God, in the name of the Lord Jesus Christ, to overcome those evil powers, and in the end directly tells Satan to be gone. It tells him to *give place to Christ, to stoop beneath the all-powerful hand of God,* and *to flee* when the petitioner invokes *the Holy and terrible name of Jesus* and goes on to ask the Lord to hear the prayer and be with the one you're praying for. And then it tells you to get them to pray another prayer with you. And then it says to sprinkle holy water at that point."

"Yes, yes, as I said I am quite familiar with the invocation. What is your question, young man?" The priest's voice had grown edgy.

Tom had pushed him far enough. "Well, I can get holy water easy enough, though I'm not sure it's legitimate. I mean, it's an online website. And Lord knows I can pray... been doing a lot of that. But the prayer in this book, has a warning on it that says it is to be said over someone else only by a priest, which I'm not." In truth, Tom wasn't afraid to use the prayers on his own, but he hoped to gain Father Gahlen's help by appealing to the priest's sense of Catholic obligation.

The man didn't respond.

"Look Father, I'm a Baptist. We believe all of us have the right to invoke the power of Christ, but I'm no spiritual cowboy. I don't think I can go this alone. And aren't most exorcisms performed with at least two or more praying, faithful believers working together? I'm not sure how my sister stands on matters of faith, and I don't know of one other clergyman—or church member for that matter—who wouldn't take months or even years of convincing to get them to believe what we're experiencing here.

And we're up against time, Father. People are dying because of this thing."

Prolonged silence developed then, but as long as the big priest stayed on the line, Tom was willing to wait him out.

At last the old cleric, voice solemn and weary, answered, "I was once like you. Sure of the strength of my faith. Confident in the knowledge of my righteous position." Father Gahlen paused. "A young woman came to me troubled by voices and evil thoughts. I was sure simple prayer and exercises of faith assigned to her would overcome whatever it was. She came week after week for over a year. Over time she displayed the vilest lewd behavior, cursing others vehemently, projecting voices that weren't hers, and languages she didn't otherwise know... doing terrible harm to herself and testing my commitment to God and the church with the slyest seductive temptations. I'd sent her to a physician and a psychiatrist and both determined whatever it was, it was not her mental or physical health. She displayed as completely normal before them."

At that point the priest's voice choked and he worked to clear his throat.

When he spoke again, the tone was husky, and hoarse. "I eventually got the approval of the church to perform the rite of exorcism. Two other priests and two nuns assisted."

Tom heard the old man blow his nose.

A huge heavy breath escaped him before he spoke again. "In the end, she died. They said it was asphyxiation. The investigation found me innocent of murder but negligent for not protecting her from gagging herself. The church took care of the scandal, and I was stripped of my position, sent off to pray and study in New Mexico for a year or so and told never to perform the rite of exorcism ever again."

The silence lasted only a few seconds this time before Tom said, "I'm sorry, Father. I had no idea. It must have been..." Words failed.

"Then one day I received a letter. There was a small parish in Normal, Illinois, that needed a pastor. I was reinstated and told to report here and forget everything else, never speak of it again. And I have held that duty faithfully, until you showed up at my door."

"I'm sorry, Father, I know it must be devastating to lose someone under your care like that. I'm sure you did all you could for that girl. But this is a desperate situation. And you have the knowledge, skills, and experience I lack."

Father Gahlen's voice was clearer and calmer when he spoke again. "I will tell you this. If you insist on facing off with this thing, you will need to isolate the subject. Get him alone, in a closed room large enough to accommodate your need, but only just so. Limit the furniture and other objects, and, you *will* need a couple of strong men. Preferably very strong. And someone else to keep an eye on the goings on who isn't necessarily there for muscle. Whoever you choose, choose them carefully. They must at least believe you are doing what's best. They don't necessarily have to believe your explanation of the demon, but they must be prepared to do whatever you say. They don't have to be clerics, if you believe. If you have the faith, Thomas Honeywell, then your faith is enough to face the devil. The real question here is, are you prepared to face the consequences of your actions, whatever they may be?"

Tom felt the confidence seeping out of him. "I know sometimes we fail, in embarrassing and painful ways, when we reach out to people in need, Father, but doesn't somebody still need to try? Especially when other lives are at stake?"

"That, young man, is precisely why I cannot, and will not help you."

The line went dead.

CHAPTER 13

Saturday, November 20, 2010

Waking early, Blaine rolled over and looked at the clock. He had half an hour till his alarm went off. *Ah hell*, he jumped out of bed. He didn't mind running in the predawn darkness.

He wasn't picking Laura up until one o'clock, but he wanted to get his workout in, and he needed to get a few things together. A thermos of coffee, a cooler of waters.

Downstairs in the kitchen, the vase of bright, fall colored flowers he'd bought for Laura waited on the counter. He raised his eyebrows and drew a breath. Enough already.

Duke interrupted Blaine's thoughts, giving one quick sharp bark and trotting to the door. He slid the glass door open as the long low tone of his home fax machine grabbed his attention. He stood over it now waiting until it finally spit out its last page. Then, pouring his coffee, he read the results from some of the lab tests he'd been waiting on.

He had submitted the jar of human eyes they'd found on Hattie Perkins' front porch, and those they'd found in Curry Porter's lair in the mountain cave. Like he feared, there was no way to identify any of the remains, specifically after all these years. DNA records didn't exist for most of the victims, and eyes preserved in hundred-proof moonshine for thirty or forty years left little to work with. But there was some possible suggested age and race information on the victims, probably all white, probably all young—early teens to early twenties. Nothing he hadn't already figured on.

He flipped to the next document. It revealed the only thing he'd wanted to know about the hound dog's condition. Chemical analysis indicated the creature that had urinated on it had to be a wolf, but the notes politely reminded the sheriff there were no wolves in northwestern North Carolina. The only ones in the state were the small red wolves raised and protected as part of a recovery program. But they were limited to the Alligator River National Wildlife Refuge on the eastern coast of the state some 300-400 miles away.

Yeah, he knew that. But these scientists had never seen the thing he'd faced in that cave. Both Laura and the preacher insisted it was an evil spirit manifesting itself as a menacing, natural creature they would all recognize and fear.

The beast had stood up on its hind legs, all of seven-foot-tall with a deep barrel chest and hollow canine hips. It had huge muscular limbs, thick claws, and coarse brownish-black fur. And it stank of animal musk. The creature he'd fought had definitely been a wolf of some kind, though not like any he'd ever encountered. Its eyes appeared to hold an eerie knowing intelligence lurking within, but that could have been his imagination.

Blaine wasn't convinced he'd faced off with a spirit being in wolf's clothing. And he still couldn't believe he'd really fought the thing hand to hand, or that when he went back into the cave to look over its fallen carcass again, it was gone, while in its place lay Curry Porter's wasted body. Blaine was a sensible man, but he had no sensible explanation for what he'd witnessed.

He tossed the papers on the counter, strapped on his service pistol, and went to meet Duke outside, his troubled mind preoccupied as he started his morning run. He needed to come up with a plan of action. Some way to get Loy to come in and get rid of that—whatever it was—before anyone else got hurt. He'd start with Tom Honeywell. Nobody else would believe what he'd seen, especially not the feds. And his own men? Maybe Adam Richardson.

Soon, however, the pounding of his own feet drowned out his worries, and his thoughts turned to Laura. Images of her in his arms the other night, looking up at him with those gentle green eyes made his groin react despite himself. And the memory of the smell of her freshly washed, honey-colored hair made his stomach feel light. He pushed through it, and he'd do the same later. At least he'd try.

Time crawled. Laura had risen early and made breakfast for Aunt Hattie, then put on a pot of ham, green beans, and potatoes for later. Cayley could heat it up for herself and the elderly woman for dinner. There was soup and salad fixings for lunch, along with Hattie's own old-fashioned-recipe *hamburg barbecue*, and there was always a pie of some kind or other in the fridge. Pie baking was one thing Aunt Hattie insisted on doing herself, even now.

Cayley, who was fast becoming more like family than an employee, would be there by noon and Laura could get her shower and get dressed then. For now she sat on the sofa watching a mind-numbing talk show. Everything else was ready; she'd picked out her clothes for... *the afternoon...* she reminded herself, attempting to avoid the idea that this was a date, even in her thoughts.

She'd spent another night tossing and turning over dreams and visions, not to mention the restless anticipation about the day ahead with Blaine. As a result, the drone of the TV host's voice was having a hypnotic effect. Laura stared unseeing at the screen and her eyelids drooped. She found herself drifting further and further into the picture, passing through a haze of people and lights, and electronic buzzing, and on into the deep forests beyond Aunt Hattie's walls.

An ethereal figure vaporized ahead of Laura. The young woman's dark reddish-brown hair billowed around her, creating the idea of a strong breeze though Laura felt none. It was humid and dank here, and it was dark, the very air oppressive, stifling. They came to a high hill where the girl turned toward Laura. The same girl, the same hill, the same scene she'd viewed through the creature's eyes, the same one she kept seeing in dreams and visions. The young woman glared at her again and turned away, heading down the hill toward Granny Beulah's. Just when Laura was about to get close enough to see what the apparition was pointing to, someone touched her, pulling her back to reality.

"Are you alright, child?" Aunt Hattie squeezed Laura's shoulder. "Sounded like you was awful upset."

Wiping the moisture gathering at the corners of her eyes, Laura sat up. "Yeah, yeah, I'm fine. It was just... It was nothing." She yawned and stretched.

"Hmm," Aunt Hattie tilted her head, watching Laura close. "It's always hard to lose somebody, but losin' your momma that way." The elderly woman shook her head sad and slow. Then, lowering herself gently onto the sofa and regarding her niece with a wary expression, she put a hand on Laura's knee. "You *still* havin' those bad dreams? Thought you'd have got over them long ago."

Laura stopped in the middle of rubbing her eyes again. "What do you mean?"

Her aunt pulled her hand away and shook her head. "Nothin' really. Everyone has a few a' them kind a' dreams, 'specially when they're young." She averted her eyes. "But you woke most every night. Your momma would send me for a cold cloth, or to make tea or somethin', so I'm not sure what you told her about them, or if you did. I just know you took a long time to fall asleep again." She frowned. "It weren't long after they started, Robey up and decided to haul you off to Pennsylvania. I know there was more to it than them dreams, but..." she sighed and raised her brow, "...sure was an unsettlin' time." She pursed her lips a moment, then drew a deep breath. "But don' you worry. You always was a wiry little thing. And you're a strong woman now. You'll be fine."

Laura stood and helped the elderly woman up, pulling her into a hug. "Yes, I'll be fine. I've got you."

Aunt Hattie returned her hug with more strength than she'd shown in days. Laura leaned back to look at her, pleased at the color in her cheeks and the brightness of her eyes.

The quick rap followed by a jingle at the front door announced Cayley's arrival. She had a key to the house to come and go as needed, and she was twenty minutes early as usual. Popping her head in the door first, she called out, "I'm here." The rest of her lively presence followed, and she bustled in carrying several bags. "Got some fresh veggies on my way over. And I brought a couple of new magazines, and crossword puzzle books. I've got a ton of 'em at home. Figured we could sit and do some later." She grinned big and bright.

The girl had a contagious smile and a way about her that drew you in, made you feel better just having her around. It was easy to see how a man might be attracted to her, perhaps even despite his own obligations. Laura hoped that wasn't the connection between Tom and this girl. *But that's none of my business*, she reminded herself, again. However, it had become obvious, at least to her, that deputy Richardson had some kind of interest.

Upstairs later, Laura took a long shower and did her best to look both feminine and casual. She was no girly girl, but she wasn't a complete tomboy either. Trying to find a comfortable in-between had forever been a struggle, and now, exceptionally nervous about being alone with Blaine in this capacity, she'd changed her entire outfit twice. Nevertheless, she was ready when he knocked on the door fifteen minutes early.

Aunt Hattie took it upon herself to be the one to greet him. "T'aint lady-like to rush to answer the door to your young man. First time especially," she said.

"He's not..." Laura started to correct her aunt. But with her heart fluttering and her palms growing damp, she shook her head with a pained grin and went down the back hallway to grab a flannel shirt and hoodie.

Hattie's voice rose above the sound of the door opening. "Sheriff, always good to see you. Come on in and set a spell."

Laura heard them chatting in the living room as she put on her jacket, sheer joy in her aunt's voice. The woman was smitten with the handsome sheriff, a thing she made no effort to hide. It gave Laura time to pause and take a deep breath. She glanced at herself in the hall mirror, adjusted her shirt collar, and fluffed her hair.

Then Aunt Hattie called for her, "Laura, Sheriff's here."

Blaine rose from the dainty chintz sofa, turning his tall brawny frame toward her and reached for her hand. "Ready?"

While Laura was no wilting flower, and she certainly had an intelligent head on her shoulders, she found herself momentarily unable to answer. Her heart fluttered, and her mouth just wouldn't respond. She dropped her gaze to his broad calloused hand and reached for it in return. Giving a nod instead of speaking, she finally looked into his soft hazel eyes with their flecks of golden brown, noting the lines at their corners that added to the warm look of him. Her blood surged.

Blaine met her eyes, steady, unwavering for endless seconds until he at last cleared his throat. Then, while still holding Laura's gaze, he said, "I'll have her back before our coach turns into a pumpkin."

The elderly woman either didn't notice the interaction or pretended not to, but she cheerily wished them well and bustled them toward the door as Cayley entered the room.

Laura finally recovered her voice to address the younger woman. "You sure you have everything you need?" she asked.

"We'll be fine. Don't you worry. Nothin's gonna happen to Miss Hattie on my watch." Cayley glanced toward the pantry. She knew where the shotgun was, and how to use it.

Blaine dropped Laura's hand to place his in the small of her back as they went out to his car. Wincing inwardly at the pain in her knee, she tried hard not to limp as they walked down the porch steps.

Duke stuck his head out the open driver's side window and woofed at them. Laura rubbed the soft fur between his ears, and speaking to the dog as if he were any other friend she said, "I'm glad to see you're joining us."

Blaine opened the passenger door for her, and the dog hopped over the console into the back. When the sheriff slid into the driver's seat, he glanced her way and smiled before starting the car and turning his attention to the road. *Breathe, just breathe.* Laura quietly drew a few deep breaths, letting them out long and slow.

As they drove, she tried to focus her thoughts on the route they traveled, so she could learn more about the area, but despite her self-calming efforts, her body stayed on high alert to his presence.

CHAPTER 14

A painted wooden sign fixed between two large stacked stone pillars announced the entrance to Mt. Jefferson State Natural Area. Blaine had shown Laura around as they drove, stopping at a local craft and furniture store when she pointed it out, to let her browse. With pride in his voice, he'd kept up a conversation about the history, geography and wildlife here. His easy manner and genuine love for the land drew Laura out of her self-conscious muddle. She kept having to remind herself, it was her home state too, and she determined then to get to know the area better.

They drove up the mountain, stopping at each overlook, hiking the short trails separately. Then parking at the top next to a large pavilion in a wooded area scattered with picnic tables, they took the trail to the peak. And with Duke trotting ahead and backtracking to them repeatedly, they hiked the short trail atop the 4,684-foot elevation of Mt. Jefferson.

At every overlook Blaine pointed out the other mountains, towns, and states they could see. Besides North Carolina, both Tennessee and Virginia lay within that panoramic vista. The views of the Blue Ridge included Grandfather Mountain with its odd profile that looked like an old man's face, most visible from the highway north and east of its slopes. Blaine also pointed out Mt. Mitchell, the tallest mountain in North Carolina, and Pond Mountain, the one that lies within all three states.

Laura carried her camera in a shoulder pack. Not wanting to miss anything, she kept stopping to take shots everywhere. To his credit, Blaine remained patient while she played the tourist. But the camera could never do justice to the magnificent mountain heights nor to Laura's feeling of sensory overload.

They held hands off and on. Blaine wrapped an arm around her as they stood overlooking the mountainsides and the valleys below, even kissed her lightly on the forehead. None of it brought on the nervous jitters she'd experienced earlier. With each passing moment Laura grew more comfortable in his presence, and in his arms. The guilt tugging at her about her late husband melted away. It was true, he hadn't been gone long, but he was gone. Logic told her she could move on when she was ready.

She stumbled on a rock in the path, giving her sore knee a tweak. Blaine reached out for her. "You okay?"

Duke rushed back to circle her legs and rubbed his nose on her knee. Blaine patted the dog, then eyed Laura a long moment before saying, "Looks like you're gimping on that leg today."

"No, I'm fine. Just twisted it yesterday somehow." She avoided his eyes and moved on.

Blaine had brought along a large thermos of coffee that warmed her hands and face in the cool November air as they sat on Luther Rock later talking about everything under the sun— everything except the Porter family issues. It had been a relief, a welcome respite from the dreams, visions, and fears involving the curse James Porter had brought upon them. But she couldn't keep them at bay long.

She wished life could be simple again. Glad to have Aunt Hattie back in her life, and just as happy to have met Blaine, she had no desire to take those things back. She only wished the curse was gone, or rather that it had never existed. It was in moments like these, when life felt normal, she still had trouble believing it did. The demon beast belonged to another realm, another world, another era. Surely it had no place in reality, not now in the twenty-first century.

"Hey," Blaine said. "Penny for your thoughts?"

"Not sure you'd want to pay if you knew what they were."

"I think I can guess. I've been sitting here watching the dark clouds gather over you."

"I'm sorry," she said. "I just wish..."

They both fell silent for several minutes.

"I'm still having visions," she finally confessed. "It's not Lottie anymore. It's a dark-haired young woman. She's about twenty, give or take a little. I've never seen her before, and she had such haunting eyes. A sort of bright, whitish, grey-blue, smoky-like. You know, that kind of sultry glowing look."

Blaine raised one eyebrow, about to say something, but must have decided it wasn't important.

Laura stared off into the distance, biting her lip before she added, "There's something else about her. She looks at me like she's angry. Lottie didn't do that. But this girl looks like she's accusing me of something, like it's my fault something terrible happened to her."

Blaine rubbed his face and sighed.

Laura tried to read his mood and felt herself withdraw when she couldn't. "I'm sorry, I know this all sounds crazy, but..."

"What do you say we talk about something else for now? This is supposed to be a time for us to get to know each other, relax a little." He leaned his head to look in her eyes. "You okay with that?"

She smiled and nodded.

He stood, tossing out the last drops of coffee and twisting the lid on the thermos. Laura grabbed the paper cups and got to her feet and their eyes met. Both smiled, then he motioned for her to lead the way.

The narrow trail from Luther Rock ran along the top of the mountain through Laurel and Rhododendron still green with foliage, while fading orange and rusty red remainders clung to the oaks and maples below. Here on top of the ridge the trees looked like large bonsai, only instead of artificial pruning, their dwarfed, gnarled trunks were prevented from normal growth by the winds and weather at this altitude. They gave the forest a slightly eerie, hobbity feel.

Laura ran her hand along a knotty branch and a red squirrel above let out a fierce rolling chatter. She dodged backward, right into Blaine, who wrapped his arms around her from behind, laughing.

Then they both went quiet and still, watching the little creature scramble through the trees away from them. Blaine lingered, drawing her in tighter, and she crossed her arms over his. He responded by nuzzling her neck. Her breath grew shallow. Eyes closing, she turned her head and breathed him in, hormones surging. A light sigh escaped her, and she was ready to melt into him, until she heard the voices of other hikers approaching.

"Uh-oh, we're about to get busted," Blaine whispered into Laura's ear, and they both laughed. Then he let her go, just before a family of four appeared on the path ahead, with Duke trotting in the lead like a trail guide.

They headed down the mountain several minutes later, for dinner at a little restaurant outside of town. Nothing fancy. They were still in hiking clothes and the dog was asleep in his crate in the SUV, but the food was delicious, and the conversation flowed—until Laura's cell phone rang.

"Hello?" Defenses down, completely relaxed, Laura crashed back to earth.

"Hey Miss Laura, it's Cayley. Something outside's been making an awful racket. Miss Hattie's pale and sweaty and shaking like a tree in the wind. Tried telling her it's just an old dog at first... but she's right, it's something big, and it's getting closer. I wouldn't call you about a noise, except Miss Hattie's reacting so and I don't want to go out looking and leave her inside by herself."

"No, don't. Don't go out there. Make sure the doors and windows are locked. We'll be there as quick as we can."

CHAPTER 15

Blaine slowed the SUV as they neared the house. Its headlights piercing the darkness allowed only a limited view of the grounds, omitting their line of sight to the barn and car shed. Laura removed her lap-shoulder belt and edged forward in her seat, gripping the dash while the sheriff flipped on a spotlight mounted on the driver's side and shone it around the property.

"There," she pointed. Something large and dark slipped around the back corner of the house.

Blaine swore and slammed the SUV into park. He went for the gun he'd locked in the glove compartment, loading it quick. Then he grabbed a flashlight. Duke had woken and alerted to the danger as soon as they pulled up, growling low, the hair on the ridge of his scruff rising slowly in response, but the sheriff didn't let him out.

To their left, Cayley stepped out on the porch, raising the shotgun as Hattie appeared just behind her. Laura's heart dropped. She jumped out of the SUV, heading for them on the run. "No, go back," Laura yelled. Fear and desperation driving her, she ordered, "Inside! Get back inside."

Laura reached the porch steps as a low, malicious snarling sounded nearby—too near. The sound settled into a heavy, scratchy breathing for several seconds before turning into a rolling, guttural growl. The creature must have slunk up from the far corner of the house in the few seconds it took Laura to get from the car to the steps. Blaine stopped, halfway to the garage and turned, shining the flashlight back toward the house.

Cayley and Hattie stood unmoving, as if frozen in place, while the creature appeared at the end of the porch, rising on its hind legs. It stood breathing heavily, its massive chest rising and falling, its breath streaming out in hot steaming puffs. In the porch light

Laura could see Loy's eyes in the beast's face, begging forgiveness even as the creature shifted its chin left and right. Its thick neck cracked in proud resistance to the meek, gentle soul it tormented.

Shots rang out. Blaine fired at the same time as Cayley, and the creature tumbled backward off the porch, stretching in reaction to pain from behind at the same time. The beast snapped and growled, struggling to maintain its footing. A battle it won in an instant, the vicious snarling gave way to a keening howl, growing faint as the beast disappeared back into the darkness.

It was over in seconds. The creature had simply been overwhelmed by fire power for the moment. It would be back again, and again, and again, until they did something to overcome its evil once and for all.

Laura sagged.

Aunt Hattie gasped, "Good Lord, what was that thing?" She hadn't yet seen the beast in all its ferocious terror. She stood now looking at Laura, a hand to her chest, shaking, her face pale.

Laura climbed the steps. Arms and legs heavy she reached for her aunt, encircling the elderly woman's shoulders. It was time she knew. "That... was Loy. He's alive and he's been stalking me ever since I got back. But," she struggled to find words, "he's not entirely himself. Not since Curry died in the cave."

Aunt Hattie swayed on her feet and Laura pulled her in closer. The elderly woman laid a trembling hand on Laura's arm. "Oh, you poor girl." Then she raised it to her mouth and mumbled behind it, "Oh my, that poor boy."

Pulling back a few inches, studying her aunt's face, Laura suddenly realized the other woman already knew. She must've always known about the creature and the Porter family's connection. Of course she would, she'd lived here all her life—all their lives. In fact, Hattie had been here long before any of them, including Loy, Curry and Glen. The stalwart elderly woman might be meek and gentle and God-fearing, but that didn't mean she wasn't wise to the evil in her world.

Laura looked up then catching Cayley's eye, and she realized at once the CNA knew as well. Again, she recognized the girl had been born and raised here. It seemed nothing was a surprise to anyone here but her. Some people might choose not to accept or believe the stories, but if they grew up here, they knew.

Blaine called his office to report the incident as the women stood watching. Now he climbed the steps, quickly ushering them into the house. "Let's get inside, ladies," he spoke as he reached for the downward pointed shotgun, pulling it gently from Cayley's hands. "Thanks for the backup, but I'll take that now," he said.

Inside, Laura helped Aunt Hattie settle onto a chair in the kitchen and ran cool water over a towel. Cayley stepped in to take over and Blaine pulled Laura aside.

"I have a couple deputies coming out. We'll stay through the night, but I doubt it'll be back. He'll know we're ready for him now. We won't go off hunting that thing in the dark, but first thing in the morning, we'll follow the trail." Blaine looked like a man trying to form a new plan. Nothing was working, bullets didn't keep it down. At least not a limited few. "I'll have to go into the office in the morning. Check with animal control about tranquilizers. We need to go after this thing like the wild animal it is."

Laura gave a deep sigh. "But, what about Loy? It's not his fault this thing is after him. He's just so... childlike. He can't help his condition."

"I'm sorry, Laura, but your uncle's safety is secondary at this point. We've got to put a stop to all this before anybody else gets hurt."

CHAPTER 16

Sunday, November 21, 2010

The night passed without further incident. Blaine slept on the couch after his turn on the night-watch, and Duke chose to sleep in Laura's room on the rug beside her bed. She made breakfast for everyone before the sheriff left.

The other deputy would be replaced soon, but there would be someone there for the foreseeable future.

Blaine kissed Laura on the forehead before he left, asking her to stay close. She didn't tell him about her plans to visit her grandmother later. But she needed to see Beulah, especially now. Besides, Aunt Hattie had settled down after a restless hour or so last night, and she appeared to be fine this morning, and Cayley promised to stay the day.

Beulah must have seen Loy again by now. Surely, he'd have made his way home at some point. Laura thought she'd be able to get her grandmother to open up to her about whatever she might know if they could just sit down and talk. Maybe she could even convince the elderly woman to help get Loy to surrender. Besides, the Porter home was close, no more than five miles.

Laura sat now drinking coffee with Cayley and Aunt Hattie as she thought, trying to determine how best to approach her grandmother.

Moments later Aunt Hattie rose and straightened her back. It was late morning and she was due for her nap. She yawned big and exclaimed, "Goodness me. I think I'm sleeping more than not these days, but I surely need to get a few winks in."

The CNA started to get up to follow, but Aunt Hattie waved her off. "You stay sittin'. I kin get myself up the stairs just fine. You two set and enjoy each other's company awhile."

Both women silently observed Aunt Hattie's progress, and then shared an approving smile.

Switching gears instinctively, Laura asked, "So you grew up here?" When Cayley only nodded, Laura prodded further. "And you left for a while? Is that right?"

Again the girl nodded, but she added, "A couple years. Not long after I graduated high school. Did my CNA training in Raleigh. Thought about becoming a nurse, but I..." she paused, hesitating. "Things were a bit tough just then, so I took the shortest, easiest course first. Thought maybe I'd go on and become a nurse later. Just never seem to find the time—or the money." She looked away and sighed before adding, "When I finished..." and she hesitated again, "...everything, I decided to come back here. It was home."

The girl had a habit of shaking her head, as if at her own thoughts. Cayley rose and deposited her coffee cup in the sink. "I need to go over Miss Hattie's med list and double-check things. So if you'll excuse me."

Laura nodded. "I'm going out for a little while. I shouldn't be too long." Not sure how much she should tell the other woman, she decided not to reveal where she was going.

The look on Cayley's face told her that the CNA already had some idea, but she avoided eye contact and took her flannel shirt and hoodie from the wall hook.

The pitted and pocked, two-story white clapboard stood spotlighted by the sun. The early morning rain had stopped, leaving behind small droplets that sparkled on the windows. Branches lay scattered about, while leaves blown in by the winds gathered in the corners and piled up against the house. The smell of wet earth hung in the air.

Laura approached Beulah's front door and halted, listening, glancing around. An old, heavy iron, triangle dinner bell hung on the porch post to her left. Laura imagined Beulah ringing it to bring her young sons in for supper. Probably could've heard it for miles. She wondered then if maybe even the creature somewhere off in a distant cave could hear that thing. She shuddered and looked out toward the mountain.

Her grandmother's house sat in a clearing in the woods, but the trees held sway here, casting long shadows at all hours of the day. They gathered around the place, slowly inching closer with each passing year, as though the forest was bent on reclaiming the whole property, while the mountain behind it swelled like a huge dragon ready to descend on its remains.

The dilapidated barn used as an all-purpose garage, wood shed, and animal shelter stood to the right. Its blackened wood planks, shrunken from age, left gaps that revealed only darkness within.

A pile of ruins several yards beyond the barn brought a vision of an old chicken coop and an outhouse. Laura hadn't recalled any childhood memories connected to this house before. She must have been here when she was a child, but she hadn't even thought of the possibility until now.

Her breathing shallow, Laura dropped her head as that familiar crawling, creeping feeling washed over her. She had a feeling she knew a lot more about this place than she consciously recalled. She glanced left with a wary eye, toward the opposite corner of the old clapboard—there was a root cellar laying just out of sight around that side of the house. The sudden thought of it now made her shudder.

The forest pressed in around her vision, and her face grew warm, her hands clammy. She bit her lip and held her breath, listening... but except for the twittering of birds, nothing disturbed the peaceful calm. *Deceivingly peaceful.* She drew a sharp breath, shaking off the thought, and knocked.

She waited a minute and tried again, harder. The sound echoed around her, loud and hollow. Another moment or two and Laura heard the familiar shuffling inside before the door creaked open and a wrinkled, leathery face appeared in the tiny gap.

"Granny, it's Laurie Allen." The volume of her greeting rousted a bird perching on the rain spout overhead, sending it skittering away with a squawk.

Laura eyed the woods with an involuntary cringe.

"Eh?" The woman put a hand to one ear. "Speak up. What's yer business?"

Laura leaned in close to the woman's cupped ear and raised the volume of her response even further. "It's me, Laurie Allen. I just came by to visit awhile if you're up to it."

"Ooh. My Glen's girl." Her grandmother stepped back, drawing the door a narrow crack wider so Laura had to pass through sideways. "Go on in the kitchen then. I was just fixin' to have a moon pie and a cup a' coffee." The tiny, bent woman closed the door with a thud that made Laura jump.

In the kitchen, Granny Beulah gestured vaguely toward the cupboard area above and to the left of the sink. "Get me that box, up there, first shelf." Then she turned over two clean coffee cups from a set of four already out on the table, and shuffling slowly, headed for the coffee pot. The completely blind, elderly woman crossed the space back to the table and poured both cups full without spilling a drop, then returned the pot to its base. "Sit down then, chil'," she commanded as she lowered herself into a chair. "Open up them moon pies."

Laura obeyed, even to the point of getting herself one, though she normally tried to avoid sweets. She hadn't had a moon pie since she was eight years old. She chased the marshmallow filled, milk chocolate covered, crunchy cookie with a swallow of hot, black coffee.

Beulah ate in silence, her blind stare fixed on an undefined spot on the green Formica table top. Laura had almost decided the elderly woman had forgotten she was there when Beulah snapped her head up, aiming that blank glare at her, and shot out, "Heared you was comin' back to stay." Then her grandmother shook her head and dropped her chin before adding, "Reckon it ain't over yet."

"Uh," Laura fumbled for words.

"Preacher's wife, 'Lizbeth, came by t'other day." Her grandmother spoke in disconnected staccato sentences. "Brings meals once a week." She got quiet again. "Talks a mite. But she's good company."

Laura waited, not wanting to interrupt.

"My Loy..." her voice broke and she cleared her throat hard. Then seconds later, tears formed in her milky eyes and spilled over as her head sank into her chest, and the old woman's shoulders convulsed.

Laura reached for Beulah's hand, realizing again the depth of love this enigmatic woman must have for her sons, her kin. Now the older woman grasped Laura's hand in both of her thin bony ones, squeezing hard and releasing.

Wiping a tear from her own eye, Laura said, "I'm so sorry." She grappled for words to soothe her grandmother's pain. She wanted to reassure her that maybe they still had a chance to rescue Loy. But she didn't want to give false hope. She ventured to ask, "Granny, have you seen him since he disappeared from the cave?"

Beulah lifted her chin, tipping her head away from Laura as if looking off into the corner. She spoke with her face turned. "No. Ain't showed hisself to me." Then in a burst of vehemence she commanded, "You mind you don' go gittin' yer*self* kil't. That thing's been after Porter blood since long 'fore you was born. It ain't ever gonna quit." The woman stared straight ahead, and her face darkened. "You tell that brother a' yours, too. You hear me? Bein' a preacher ain't gonna protect 'im none."

A sudden thought occurred to Laura as she listened. Something she'd never considered. She hesitated to ask now, afraid the elderly woman would shut down and refuse to answer, but she had to know. "Granny, have *you* ever seen the creature?"

Beulah got up, put her empty cup in the sink and stood with her back to Laura. "Done said too much."

Laura stepped up beside the tiny woman and put her arm around her grandmother's shoulders. "Granny," she said it softly, gently, "it must have been so hard for you. Losing your husband so young. Trying to raise and protect your sons by yourself all these years."

The old woman's shoulders sagged. "You don' know the half."

Laura gave her grandmother a gentle squeeze and laid her cheek against the woman's hair.

Beulah pulled away and headed for the old hutch. She opened the lower doors and wrestled out a large stack of photo albums. Without a word, she shuffled back to the kitchen table and laid them out before she settled her aging body back into her seat. "Them brown ones. They's the oldest. Got pictures of my man, Ervin, in 'em."

Opening the thickest volume, Laura found a lot of faces she didn't recognize, but soon she came upon baby pictures of her father, and his brothers Curry and Loy with their birthdates and full names.

Granny somehow seemed to know what had drawn her attention. "Got all the baby pictures, birth certificates, baptismals too. 'Course Loy weren't never baptized. He couldn' a' tol' you what it was for, so the preacher said it weren't no point. Good Lord takes care a' them as got no understandin'."

Granny Beulah reached across the book and closed it. Then apparently counting as she went, she flipped it open again until she found what she wanted. She felt the page, her fingers coming to rest in the top left corner on the photo of a man in hunting gear with a rifle barrel clutched in his fist, the butt end on the ground. The man's right foot sat on the top side of a large dead black bear.

Beulah's eyes teared and in a voice weary from years of sorrow, she said, "That'd be my man, Ervin. He died 'fore Loy was born." Her unseeing gaze fixed somewhere in the distant past and she went on. "That there was the biggest black bear ever seen in these parts. He fig'rd he'd got the creature folks'd been so feared of." She turned her face toward Laura before she spoke again. "Tol' him he was wrong." She paused, her head shaking in quick short tremors.

Laura sat quiet, sensing her grandmother wasn't finished. The old woman's right eye twitched, her upper lip was damp, and her face went a shade paler.

Beulah wiped at the moisture before she spoke. "Lotta folks was wrong." She got quiet again, clasping her hands together, squeezing. Then she lifted her chin, bringing her eyes level with Laura's. "Some said the creature was one a' them bigfoots. Pure foolish talk. Aint' no sech thing. I seen this beast. I know'd what it was, and it weren't no bear, and it weren't no ses-quatch neither."

Laura's pulse quickened. If her grandmother had seen the demon, it had to have been a very long time ago. Beulah had been mostly blind for the latter half of her life.

Laura put a hand on her grandmother's knee. "It must have been awful living in fear of that thing. But, what about your husband? Did he ever..." she hesitated, searching for the right words, "was he... like other Porter men?"

Beulah's head came up a few inches before she spoke. "My man weren't one given to temptations." Her jaw jutted out, and her chest rose. "He was straight laced, my Ervin. Didn't cotton to moonshinin'. Stayed to hisself. Took care a' his own. Didn't go galavantin' like other men. Went to church ever Sunday mornin', tithed his ten percent faithful." The old woman let her head sink down and grew quiet.

Watching her grandmother's leathery face, Laura noted the deep wrinkles around her mouth. The woman's eyes closed, and she set her lips in a tight line.

Laura shifted in her seat and waited, but the silence became too much. "Granny?" she spoke softly.

Beulah drew in a breath and opened her eyes, turning her blind gaze on Laura again. "My Ervin's only wrong was keepin' that old bowie knife. Shoulda destroyed that thing when he come on it." She let her head sink the whole way to her chest again and finished in a low voice, "Then my Curry never would a' found it later out in that ol' shed."

Laura recalled an old photo Beulah had given her the last time she'd visited. It showed James Porter holding the bowie knife clutched tight in his fist. She also remembered it sticking out of Loy's hound dog's chest, when the creature had attacked them in the caves, and she'd seen it most recently clutched in Loy's own raised hand.

"Granny." Laura touched the old woman's arm. "I'm sorry about what's happened to your sons. I wish I'd had more time to know my daddy—and his brothers, before..." She stopped, waiting briefly for some reaction. Finally, she tried again. "Loy might come in if he thought you..."

Beulah pushed her chair back from the table with a scrape, silencing Laura. Her head shaking vigorously, she tucked her hands, one atop the other, in her lap and her whole body sank down into the seat. Her thin, age-spotted hands protruded from her pale blue flowered dress while the fringes on the hand-crocheted shawl she wore sprawled across her lap.

At last her head slowly stopped shaking, dropping so low, Laura couldn't see her face well enough to gauge her reactions. Then with her blind eyes closed, her hands still folded, Beulah murmured an old hymn Laura recognized. "Rock of Ages" came out broken, slightly out of tune and softly haunting as the elderly woman swayed.

Laura waited till her grandmother finished the song, then laid a hand on her shoulder. "Granny, I need to go, but I'd like to come back and visit you again, often." She paused, watching the older woman's face before she finished. "If that's alright with you?"

Beulah's head came up a few inches. "That'd be jus' fine."

Laura collected the albums to put them away, but Beulah reached for her arm. "You go on an' take them picture books with you. Reckon they's yours now." She laid a pale withered hand on top of the albums and patted them. "You take care of 'em," she said with finality.

Tears threatened Laura's burning eyes. Before she left, she gathered the tiny woman in a warm, firm hug. "I'll see you again, soon." She paused before adding, "I love you, Granny."

Beulah patted Laura's arm, tears glistening in her own eyes, but she said nothing more.

The elderly woman shuffled into the living room and settled herself into a recliner to nap, leaving Laura to see herself out. In the driveway, she laid the albums gently on the front passenger seat of the Toyota and paused to glance back. She thought about checking out the old root cellar. Thought about it, briefly. Then she scanned the woods and the mountain above, but all was quiet.

She'd just turned to slide into the car when she heard branches snapping and leaves rustling. She froze, holding her breath for several long seconds, waiting...

CHAPTER 17

Loy ducked out of sight. He'd left the old four-wheeler up the trail a ways and crept through the woods on foot. He hadn't stayed long, but he just had to see his momma. He was leaving the old barn shed with the gas can when Miss Laurie pulled in.

He didn't want to see her now. He'd held out so long against the creature while visiting his momma. His head hurt. His eyes burned. That was always the first sign the thing was coming.

He was working on figuring out a way to get rid of the beast for good, or at least control it. The cutting and bleeding helped. The beast left him alone while he did it anyway. Weakened it somehow, or maybe it just wanted to let him hurt himself. He didn't know for sure.

He'd figure a way to get rid of the thing, but he needed to be more careful. He didn't want to risk having that creature come on him again while he was face-to-face with Miss Laurie.

She'd been in there a long time with his momma, so he finally decided it was safe to make his way back up the mountain. But then she came out and now he was crouched low behind a big tree stump with the gas can between his knees, barely breathing, and his head hurt, real bad. His eyes burned like fire, and his chest felt like it would explode. *Noooo, noooo!*

Then again, now might be a real good time.

Miss Laurie was alone, and his momma wouldn't hear or see nothing. She'd be napping by now.

Maybe it *was* time for Miss Laurie to know all the things he knew. Or was it the creature that knew them? He wasn't sure. But, maybe it was time she faced the beast herself, seeing this was all her fault. That's what Curry had said. That's what the creature kept telling him. That's what it wanted.

Noooo! He's wrong, he's evil. He only wants to hurt Miss Laurie 'cause he hates her.

Loy never spoke directly to the creature. He feared it might give it more control, but he knew what it wanted all the same.

Gotta watch out for her. Like Glen said. You promised. Keep her safe or...

Loy pounded his head with the heel of his hand. Trying to think clear. Panting hard, trying to make the beast go away. Trying to un-mix his thoughts, untangle them from the creature inside his head. But *it* was coming. His brain hurt, his mouth was dry, and his neck was stiff.

Then he heard a car door close. He rose up just enough to look over the stump.

Miss Laurie was heading right toward him.

Loy opened his mouth to scream, but it turned into a howl. His chest rose and his eyes glowed red.

Nooooooo!

He jumped up, grabbing the gas can in one hand. Howling and screaming, he ran up the mountain away from his momma's house, away from Miss Laurie, running for dear life—hers.

CHAPTER 18

Laura ran for cover beside the old barn. Risking a look around the corner, she watched Loy, his body contorting, howling like a wild animal. With no idea how to help him, she stayed put, hoping he would gain control over the creature. But in seconds, he took off up the mountain swinging a sloshing gas can, the howl turning into a piteous cry of mingled fear and rage.

She slid to the ground by the old barn, eyes closed against the sight of Loy's torture, as the rattle-trap four-wheeler started up and rumbled away. When the sound died off, Laura finally looked up.

The sky had turned a darkling grey. The air had chilled and a damp quiet settled over the forest—the kind that deadens footfalls, brings a hush to the world, and leaves a person feeling alone. No bird twitter, no chipmunk chatter, not even a cricket chirping. The eerie cold seeped into her bones, though no breeze carried it along.

Sensing eyes on her, Laura turned to find the same girl from her vision two nights ago staring at her, hands on her hips, waiting. Her expression still hard to comprehend—condescension, disdain, accusation?

Despite the apprehension finger-walking up her spine, Laura scrambled to her feet and approached the girl. She might have been about twenty. Her smooth, fair skin created a stark contrast to her long, dark mahogany hair. With the apparition no more than two feet away, Laura could see right into those smoky, whitish blue-grey eyes. The young woman turned and led the way around the back of Beulah's house to the far side—where the root cellar door stood open.

Laura stopped. Staring down the gaping black maw, her skin grew damp and she began to tremble. Realizing she'd been here before—not just to her grandmother's, but there in that cold, dingy cellar—the crawling feeling in her spine reached her neck and scalp.

She'd been headed for potatoes. Granny Beulah had wanted a small basket full, five or six, but it was so dark in there. Laura hated the root cellar. And she'd only recently found a little girl's bones in that other cold, dark place. Now she thought she saw a shadowy bulk hunched in the corner. It began to grow, bigger and bigger as she stared open-mouthed. She'd dropped the basket and turned... but a hand fell on her shoulder, gripping hard.

The lithe figure of the apparition in front of Laura descended the steps into the blackness below. Some part of her resisted the urge to follow, her chest constricted. The darkness, the stifling air familiar. It stung her nose and scratched her throat. The child inside screamed, "Run," but her adult mind insisted she find out what gave her such irrational fear.

The shadow grew and stood over her. She couldn't move. Her feet just wouldn't cooperate. Then it leaned down and whispered in her ear, its breath fouled with moonshine. "You gonna stay here with me now, child. Your daddy done tol' your momma too much. They got to realize, they can't go agin the beast." Then the shadow grabbed her arm, starting to back into the cellar with her when a shaft of light caught his face.

Entranced by her own morbidly troubling memories, and compelled by a macabre sort of awe, Laura descended the stone steps now. Dim light from outside filtered in and her eyes struggled to adjust as she felt her way along the wall, feet shuffling. She blinked several times and the small space came into clearer view. The air in the old root cellar was thick with a damp, moldy scent, though there were no potatoes left anymore. There probably hadn't been any stored here in years, but there *was* something in that far corner.

Uncle Curry's face was twisted and dark, his teeth glittering yellow in a nasty sneer. "You did it, didn't you?" she'd cried out.

Suddenly fear clawed at grown-up Laura's throat. The air turned heavy, her limbs sagged. She crept forward, each step drawing all her strength. Her feet dragged, barely leaving the dirt floor. When she finally got close enough to reach out for the thing, it turned out to be a dirty, dingy patchwork quilt with large dark blotches.

Despite the warning bells going off in her mind, she lifted the corner, but she leaned over so far her weight shifted, and her feet slipped out from under her on the clammy earthen floor. In the next instant she tumbled forward and landed on something sharp and hard. Something stared at her with a morbid, empty gaze. Something she'd never wanted to encounter, ever again.

Laura screamed.

CHAPTER 19

Sitting on the front steps of her grandmother's house, Laura clamped her upper arms in both hands and shivered. Beulah, who despite being nearly deaf had heard her screams, sat on a rocking chair on the porch behind Laura.

The sheriff and several deputies arrived at the same time. Several cars coming to a skidding stop, one after another, drew Laura out of her daze. She stood then, and waited for Blaine to approach.

He stopped within arms-length, looking down at her. "You okay?" When she only shrugged, he asked, "Where's the root cellar?"

Laura nodded her head to the right. Still without speaking, she turned and led the way with heavy steps to the open cellar door. The cold musty air wafted up from below and she shuddered. Staring down into the damp darkness again, her body swayed unsteadily. "In the far corner."

Blaine switched on a flashlight and stepped into the black hole. Adam Richardson followed suit while the other two deputies waited with Laura. She could hear the men's voices below but not what they were saying until Blaine exclaimed clearly, "What the hell?" Followed in short order by, "Jesus, God, no!"

Loy leaned his pale frame against a giant oak tree, bony fist grinding into the bark. They'd found her. Miss Laurie had found her. *'Course she did.* She knew the old root cellar well as he did.

But this one hadn't been found before now. Though he'd taken good care of her too, just like Lottie. Only this one weren't special the way Lottie was. But she'd always been real nice to him when he'd stop in at the 7-Eleven.

Tears trickled down his dirty face leaving almost white trails. But now the law had found this one. And soon they'd figure out who she was—and what he'd done to her, and then that big sheriff would have his hide. They wouldn't understand he couldn't save her, so he'd done the only thing he could think of to save the part of her body Curry would have taken and kept.

CHAPTER 20

Monday, November 22, 2010

Once again, Laura found herself sitting on Aunt Hattie's front porch, rocking—arms across her stomach, fingers interlaced, thumbs encircling each other in rhythm continuously. It was early afternoon and she'd waited for him all morning.

At last, Blaine pulled into the driveway and she tensed. She still had no idea what had caused his strange behavior last night. True, it was a gruesome discovery even this many years later, but the sheriff wasn't a man to react to dead bodies out of fear or horror. Yet, he'd questioned her only briefly, his face ashen. And then, hands shaking, he ushered her into her car to leave, sending a deputy to follow her home. He hadn't looked her in the eye or spoken to her personally from the moment he'd set foot in that cellar.

She'd interrupted the planning stages of a man-hunt for Loy, she knew that, but that wouldn't explain his odd reaction. Could he simply be that angry with her for going against his advice and leaving the house without clearing it with him first? Surely not. She was an adult. She had the right to go anywhere she wanted anytime she wanted without his permission, and if he thought different... well, like the old folks used to say, *he had another think coming.*

Hat in hand, he climbed the steps and stopped with one foot on the top. Running a hand over his buzzcut, he raised his eyes to hers, his gaze penetrating. Laura looked away, certain she was in some sort of trouble but not sure how serious.

Blaine cleared his throat. "So, what made you go into that root cellar? Was *it* there?" His voice held a biting edge.

She shook her head. "Didn't see it, but Loy was there. He was out in the shed. Then he ran off up the mountain when he realized I'd spotted him. I'm not sure, but I think he was fighting the thing off."

Blaine's face grew hard. His jaw muscles flexed, his mouth drawing in a tight line. Laura decided now wasn't the time to plead Loy's case.

"But it wasn't him that led me there. It was that girl I told you about. The one with the smoky blue-grey eyes."

Blaine's mouth opened slightly with a sudden outward push of air, like he'd been punched in the gut. "You should've told me he was there. Jesus, we could've gone after him." He stared hard at her. "You've got to stop trying to protect him and let me do my job."

He crossed the porch with heavy steps and settled onto the other rocking chair, hooking his hat on his knee. Then he stared off into the distance several minutes without speaking.

Laura watched him, waiting. The hardness melted away, replaced by a look of deep, silent torment. His shoulders sagged, and he finally looked her way. "Your vision. Describe her to me again. In as much detail as you can remember."

Her own burst of self-righteous indignation spent itself out and she swallowed hard before she spoke. "She was taller than me. Long, thick, dark hair with a reddish tinge, kind of like mahogany. And her eyes were this sultry bluish-grey. She was fair skinned. A smooth, creamy-like complexion. She had on one of those thin cotton summer dresses, the kind that flares from the waist down, a pretty yellow one with tiny flowers." Laura looked away, her brow creased in thought. "And she wore a necklace. I don't remember what was on it, but the chain was gold."

"It was a heart and key pendant."

"What? You mean you found one with the body?"

Blaine reached into his shirt pocket and brought out the corroded necklace, holding it up, staring at it with an odd sort of pained fascination.

100

"She saw that in a secondhand shop one time. Wanted it awful bad, so I scrounged up the fifty bucks and got it for her for Christmas that year. We were still in high-school." He reached into his pocket again. "Found this, too." He produced a plain gold wedding band with engraving around the inside. "She wanted us both to have the anniversary date engraved on them along with another little heart and key." He handed the jewelry to Laura. "Mine's in a box somewhere in my stuff." His jaw flexed. "Quit wearing it after a couple years when she didn't show up."

Laura's eyes grew wide while Blaine's pooled with unshed tears.

"What are you saying?"

He looked away, swallowing visibly several times before he spoke. "It was her. My wife. Lilly." He stabbed the sentences out as though he couldn't believe his own voice. Then he rubbed his face and heaved a sigh. "I thought she'd left. I was sure, because she took a suitcase. But looking back, it wasn't enough for her to leave home with for good. She was probably just going off for a few days or something when he..."

He stopped and leaned forward in the rocker, hands gripping both arms of the chair.

"All this time I thought... And now I find out she was just another one of your uncle's victims. She couldn't have come home if she'd wanted to."

Laura cringed. With the pain in his voice and his haunted expression, she longed to reach out to him. He leaned forward. Elbows on his knees, hat in his hands now, staring hard at the old wood porch floor. It made Laura's heart hurt.

Then his phone rang, and he stood to answer. Listening a few seconds, he closed the conversation with whoever it was in a single sentence. "Alright. I'll take care of it." He turned to Laura as she rose to join him. "I have to go. But there'll be a deputy here round the clock."

He stopped and eyed her several seconds, searching her face. She looked away before asking, "What are you planning to do?"

"I still have a crew searching Beulah's. See if there's any other clues to Loy's whereabouts. We'll finish up there by tomorrow morning. Then I'll organize a search and we'll go out after him. Right now, I've got other duties to tend to." He took Laura by both arms and turned her toward him. "But we need to talk eventually. About us."

They shared a long look before he turned and pressed his hat down snug, descending all four porch steps in two strides.

Laura found Aunt Hattie puttering around in the kitchen. There was nothing that really needed doing, but she needed to find something to keep her occupied. The elderly woman hated sitting around being lazy, as she put it, early in the day. She always said it was the best time to get things done. Cayley was accommodating, jumping right in to help the older woman while keeping a watchful eye on Hattie's condition. She assured Laura, her aunt was steadily improving and would be better off getting up and about, doing as much as she proved able.

The two had just put an apple pie in the oven and set the timer when Laura entered.

Cayley reached back to untie the apron she'd borrowed as she spoke. "I'm heading out in a few minutes. Think you two will be okay for now? I was planning on the rest of the afternoon off."

Laura turned to her. "Sure, we'll be fine." She hesitated a moment and added, "I'm sorry, I forgot. I guess we've been keeping you awfully busy." She studied Cayley's face, realizing the nurse aide spent much of her time here with Aunt Hattie, suddenly wondering what the other girl's life might be like outside her caregiving duties. Laura had been unwittingly selfish.

"Oh no, it's not that. I just have a few things to do and some errands to run. I'll be back tomorrow as usual." The younger woman waved a hand like it was no big deal. "Call me if you need to. Really. It's okay."

Laura stood at the door waving as Cayley backed her car around and left. She wondered again about the relationship between Tom and this girl. Laura's thoughts were interrupted by the scoot of a chair. She closed the door, then went back to the kitchen and took her place at the table.

Aunt Hattie was sitting down to cookies and coffee. Motioning to the oatmeal chocolate chips, she urged Laura, "Help yourself."

"Okay, but I'm telling you, I'm going to weigh a ton if I keep eating like this."

"Nonsense. You always was a little slip of a thing. Couldn't put no weight on you no matter how much I tried."

Laura thought for a moment, then she shifted forward in her chair and asked, "Speaking of my childhood, did I ever visit Granny Beulah back when I was little?"

Aunt Hattie laid her cookie in the crook between her coffee cup and saucer. Her face went solemn and she looked away across the room at first, vacantly staring at nothing. At last she turned her gaze back to Laura and answered apologetically, "She *was* your grandmother, and you were her only grandchild."

"I'm not accusing you of anything wrong. It's just..." Laura bit her lip, picturing herself cowering in the root cellar as she focused hard on a spot on the table top. Finally, she said, "It's just, I keep getting these quick little flashes of the place, like memories I'd long forgotten."

Aunt Hattie met Laura's eye, brows drawn. "Beuly used to like to have me drop you there sometimes. Especially when her sight got worse. Robey worked at a diner over in West Jefferson, and I kept you most of the time 'cause your momma preferred it that way. But Beuly insisted she had a right, and Robey allowed for it now and then." The elderly woman dropped her gaze and fell silent, brooding.

Laura waited a moment, then pressed on. "I think I was in that root cellar of hers before. It's one of the reasons I was drawn to it. But I don't remember much about it. Just trying to go after potatoes, and being scared." She didn't elaborate on the fears she held of that dank place, or her memories of feeling so afraid of her Uncle Curry. And she couldn't remember what happened after she'd run.

Aunt Hattie breathed deep and let it out slow, nodding her head. "You was eight years old, and it was just a few weeks after you'd found Lottie Edwards' bones under that cabin porch."

"Did I go there often? To Granny Beulah's? I just don't remember clearly."

"Mm-hmm, you went pert near every week for a visit. I'd drop you off and come back a few hours later to pick you up. You got along good with her, always seemed to enjoy bein' around her, but..." She paused, then looked at Laura. "You never did like your Uncle Curry much, and Loy sort of scared you, bein' strange like he was. But you still wanted to go visit your granny."

Laura tried hard to raise an image in her mind of those childhood visits with her grandmother, but she could never get more than a quick flash and a momentary sense of familiarity, and always along with something akin to panic.

"I figured it wasn't Beulah's fault the day you ran off from there and got lost. You were awful afraid a' the dark. Beuly didn't realize it or she wouldn't a' sent you into that cellar. But your momma wouldn't let you go back after that 'cause it'd made things ten times worse. And then it wasn't long before your momma packed you up and left here."

"Made what worse?" Laura leaned in and crossed her arms on the table.

Aunt Hattie hesitated, looking away briefly before answering. "Those dreams you'd been havin', wakin' in the night screamin' like somethin' was after you ever since you found Lottie Edwards. If Beulah'd known that, I don't think she'd a' sent you down there, but your momma kept it all private. Then she blamed your granny when you got worse right away. She always feared somethin' happened to you down in that cellar, somethin' you couldn't even speak of."

The elderly woman shifted uneasily in her seat, eyes turning away toward a top corner of the kitchen. Laura followed her gaze as if expecting to find further explanation hanging there in midair.

Then Aunt Hattie shook her head and brought her eyes back to Laura's face. "You kept sayin' you were seein' Lottie, and she was talkin' to you 'bout a big mean, evil creature. You claimed to see other girls like her too—scary, bloody ones reachin' out for you. Then, when your momma would ask you about the cellar, tears would roll, and you'd hide your face in her bosom. Got so you couldn't sleep alone. It was probably part a' the reason Robey figured to get you away from here." She dropped her gaze, "That... and your daddy."

Laura drew her lip in and bit down thinking. Seconds later she said, "I remember being afraid of dark closed spaces. Still am mostly. And I recall dreaming I was being chased or followed sometimes, but I thought everybody had that."

"I don't know about other folks, but it was a bad time for you. You'd wake up talkin' about big scary shadows, ghost girls, and terrible monsters."

Laura's suspicions were right. This wasn't the first time she'd encountered these, what? Apparitions, spirits—ghosts? She still had trouble getting her mind around the idea that these things were real. Wait, but then that meant she... *God, no.*

Laura's mind shouted at her. *You could have stopped this long ago.*

If only she'd understood then, but she was just a child. Yet if she had figured it out back then and done something about it, Blaine's wife might still be alive. And who knows how many other innocent young women? But whenever she'd thought about it, there had always been in the pit of her stomach an awful yawning dark fear. So, she'd simply pushed it aside, chose not to think about it—for years. Now at least she knew why.

As for how well she'd been handling things since she came back, she'd been woefully sluggish about getting involved with the paranormal, or whatever this was. Laura hadn't even told Aunt

Hattie about the renewed dreams and visions she'd been having, or exactly what she suspected they were up against with the creature. She'd convinced herself it was better not to worry her aunt any further.

Truth was, she'd allowed her own apprehensions to keep her from accepting the possibility that her uncle's dead victims were reaching out to her. She'd let her fears keep her from acting sooner, even when she began to realize what was happening. And her uneasy reservations had cost her father's *and* her mother's life. Protecting Aunt Hattie from the knowledge had been unnecessary, pointless. Especially considering she knew so much more about what had happened in the first place.

Laura interrupted her own thoughts to ask, "But you said I got lost. I don't remember that. How did you find me?"

"Truth is, we didn't find you. Loy did."

Laura's mouth fell open, her eyes wide.

"Carried you here on foot. Wrapped you in his own coat, brought you to our door and set you down. You ran to your momma, and the only thing that boy could say was, '*Okay, she okay,*' just like that." The elderly woman shook her head again at the memories. "Your momma checked you over good, but you weren't hurt, and he just turned and left."

"Seems like Beulah would remember all this, but she's never let on. In all the times I've been there, she's never said a word about it." Laura thought a moment before continuing, "Do you think she'd cover for Loy now? I mean if she knew where he was and could get in touch with him, do you think she'd hide him, keep him away from us?"

"Maybe. Can't say for sure. She's always been the private sort, especially when one a' her own was in trouble."

Laura leaned back in her chair. "But if she could be convinced he's in more trouble by hiding out than he would be if he came in and talked to someone..." she trailed off to think a moment. Then she said, "Beulah looks forward to Elizabeth's visits, talks to her quite a bit. Maybe..." Her mind made up, Laura excused herself, promising to make dinner later.

Dialing the phone as she climbed the stairs, Laura closed her bedroom door softly when Tom answered. She explained the situation and added, "It was Blaine's wife."

"Holy... Are you sure?"

"Well, he's sure, so that makes it pretty definite. They're still searching Granny's house and grounds, but Blaine knew the jewelry with the... body."

"Did Beulah know about it?"

"No, but I think she knows more than she's telling me about how to find Loy." She hesitated before adding, "And I believe there might be a chance Elizabeth can get her to tell us."

"What makes you think that?"

"She told me Elizabeth visits often and it sounds like she trusts her—more than you or me, maybe. It's worth a try. We've got nothing else."

A deep sigh on the other end of the line told her the preacher wasn't keen on involving his wife, but Laura pressed on. "Lives have been lost, Tom, and others may be at stake, including yours and mine. Surely Elizabeth would want to help."

"I'd rather keep her out of this."

He got quiet and Laura waited, wondering if his reasons had anything to do with the fact Cayley was here in the middle of it all.

"All right. But if she gets hurt..."

Laura hung up. Biting her lip, worrying the cell phone cover with her thumb, she realized, if anything did happen to her sister-in-law, it would be one more person she'd be responsible for allowing the demon to harm. But she could think of no other alternative.

CHAPTER 21

Tuesday, November 23, 2010

Blaine spotted the opening in the floor where one of his deputies had popped up a few loose boards. Eyes avoiding the evidence sitting on the dresser, he glared at the empty hiding place several long seconds. At last he turned and lifted the small mason jar by the ring around the lid, keeping it at arm's length. His stomach lurched. He shoved the jar at the nearest deputy and made for the door.

Outside he hung over the side of the porch, one hand on an upright support, heaving. When he finally stopped retching, he groaned in agony and punched the post, tearing his knuckles, smearing blood across the wood. The pain felt good.

God damn it, this is all my fault.

The other deputies skirted around the sheriff as they left the house carrying the evidence, but Adam Richardson stepped up beside him, waiting.

Blaine spit off to the side and cleared his throat, wiping damp eyes on his shirt sleeve. "Make sure the..." he choked on the word, "...*evidence* gets to the lab. And wrap things up here. We've got enough."

"Sure thing, Sheriff." Adam continued to nod, standing with his hands in his pockets.

"What?" Blaine demanded, the hard edge helping hold his emotions in check.

"Nothin', I guess. It's just..." Adam dropped his gaze to his feet. When he looked up again he said, "Shouldn't we go out after him? I mean, do you want me to get a few guys and head out into the mountain to look for him?"

"No." The sheriff bit the word out. "I'll be in charge of this one." He sighed, running a hand over his face before continuing, "He won't go far. Not with his momma still here." Blaine rubbed his buzz cut and replaced his hat.

He drove the few miles to Hattie Perkins' with his hands clenching and releasing the steering wheel. Duke, riding shotgun in the SUV, whined off and on and bobbed his nose at Blaine., who reached out and rubbed the dog's head. "Don't you worry, buddy. You're going to help me chase this S.O.B. down. We'll take care of him, and this so-called demon once and for all."

Pulling up in front of Hattie's place, the sheriff put the car in park and propped both arms on the steering wheel. Duke shifted his weight from one side to another and whined again until Blaine turned to follow the dog's gaze out toward the tobacco shed and the field beyond. Nothing. Loy Porter was slow, but he wasn't dumb. Wherever he was, he wouldn't likely show himself now. They'd have to run him to ground to get him—and that's just what Blaine intended to do, no matter how soft-hearted Laura was about her uncle's condition. The evidence proved he was no innocent victim.

When Laura stepped out on the porch, pausing with the door still in hand, Blaine took a deep breath and climbed out of the SUV. Duke shifted moods at the sight of her. He jumped across the seats and bounded up the steps to greet the woman, tongue lolling and tail wagging. The sheriff dropped the hard façade briefly to give a reserved smile. Despite everything going on, this woman took his breath away. When it came to her, Blaine identified with Duke's sentiments.

She looked up at him from her crouched position beside the dog, both hands lost in Duke's thick mottled fur, and smiled. Blaine's chest constricted. He was pretty sure he blushed, but he covered it by removing his hat and staring into it for a minute before lowering it to his side.

She bit her lip and looked back at Duke, giving him a quick hug before she stood to face Blaine, and his own smile faded with hers. He could feel himself stiffen against the conversation to come.

"You have time to sit down?" he asked.

They sat on the porch steps, out of earshot of Hattie and Cayley as he explained what they'd found at her grandmother's house, in Loy's own room. Laura was shaking her head like she couldn't believe him.

"They were my wife's. No mistaking that misty blue-grey."

"But you can't be sure Loy did it," she insisted. "I mean, why? Why would he take the..." she paused and looked away, "...trophy his brother would've wanted? Curry had all the rest, and he was definitely the killer. My father said so."

"Your father only told us about Lottie Edwards. He didn't give us any other information." Blaine let the comment sink in a moment, then added, "And he wouldn't have known much more because he was hiding out. He would have had no idea what Loy was doing."

"No," Laura shook her head again. "No, he wouldn't do such a thing. No way he's involved in the murders. He couldn't be, he's so, so..."

"Simple?" Blaine filled in with his own words. "Innocent?"

Her brow creased. "Yes. But not just that." She looked down, then lifted her eyes to his. "I saw him in the woods the other day and he was so tortured by that... that... beast. He was fighting it so hard, cutting himself, threatening to bleed the monster out."

He stretched back, looking down at her. "What do you mean? You saw him another time? Recently? When?"

She sighed and licked her lips. "I went for a hike up to the old Hadley cabin the other day," she hesitated, "just to have a look around, and he came in. But it wasn't him exactly."

Laura stood then, going down the steps and turning at the bottom to look up at him. "He wasn't himself. That creature was torturing him, controlling him, but not completely. I ran out and he followed. But after a few seconds he stopped and just stood there bending over, like he was hurting. Then he dropped to his knees and started screaming and cutting himself, going on about how sorry he was. I tried to talk to him, but then he just ran."

Blaine met her at the bottom of the steps and turned her to face him. He flexed his jaw, doing his best to control his fear and anger. Choosing his words carefully, he said, "He could've killed you." He drew a heavy breath. "You've got to stop interfering. This is a police investigation now and we will find him. One way or another. Please don't make this into another search and rescue. You might not come out of it alive this time."

"But," she hesitated, "I'm sure he's a victim, too. I just can't stand by and let him die because of that thing. He had nothing to do with bringing it into this hollow, and he had nothing to do with your wife's murder."

"Enough." Blaine bit the word out sharper than he intended. Trying again he said, "It's time to put a stop to this. He's threatening you and that's enough to bring him in on. Go on inside with your aunt, take care of her, and just stay out of sight till we find him."

He dropped his hands from her arms and stared down at her.

"He's not what you think. He's just not able to fight this thing off by himself." She stared back up at him, her eyes pooling with unshed tears.

Restraining his frustration and the brewing anger that stirred in his chest, Blaine tried to sound reasonable. "We can't let him wander the area anymore. We have just cause to believe he's involved in one killing at least, and there is no statute of limitations on murder."

The tears spilled over and Laura turned away. She stopped at the porch door and looked back at him. "You're wrong," she said and went in, letting the screen door slap shut.

CHAPTER 22

Tom glanced at his wife before starting the truck, her face unreadable in the wake of their conversation with Beulah Porter. Elizabeth had a way with the elderly, especially Beulah. He was pretty sure she'd convinced the other woman it would be in Loy's best interest to come in to see Tom, or at least to try to get him to. But his wife sat unmoving, her face a mask as they pulled away.

"I don't plan to hurt him." Tom tested the waters of conversation. "I'm trying to help the man."

Elizabeth turned her eyes to him without moving her head, her lips in a tight line.

"He needs help." He tried again. "Spiritual help."

She looked out the passenger side window, staring intently. "I know." Then his wife turned to him, face full of fear. "I know he does, but I'm scared for you as much as him. I'm worried you're in over your head with this. It isn't like helping someone who's just lost their way. This is... frightening."

He reached across the seat and closed his hand over hers. "I know, I know, but I'm the only one around here with the kind of knowledge to help him. And other than you and Laura, I'm the only one who believes the whole demon theory."

"Just tell me you'll stop if it looks like he's no longer... Loy." She stared him down as they sat at a stop sign. "You know what I mean."

He was about to answer when they heard the clanging of a dinner bell behind them. The two shared a wondering look before driving on.

It was still early and barely an hour later, while Tom sat at his desk reading again from the book the priest had given him. He heard the unmistakable sound, the loud warbling rumble of Loy's old four-wheeler. He rose from his chair to glance out the window. Beyond the graveyard near the woods edge, the older man was slowly making his way along the fence line.

Tom debated whether he should step outside to meet him. The last time he did, Loy had run away, but his momma had sent him this time. Tom waited a few more seconds, allowing the ATV to turn into the church parking lot before heading for the sanctuary door at the left side of the altar.

This time Loy pulled into the side parking lot and stopped in front of the preacher, eyeing him suspiciously. His clothes were dirty and tattered. The exposed skin at his forearms, wrists and balding head, was covered in scars and scratches, now crusted over with dried blood, and he was filthy. He shut the four-wheeler off and climbed down, dropping his head without speaking.

"Hey, Loy." Tom tried to keep his voice light and friendly. "It's good to see you." He bent his own head trying to catch the man's eye, but Loy refused to meet his gaze. "I was hoping to have a chance to talk with you about a few things. Maybe you could come inside." Tom motioned to the church. "Just for a little while."

Loy raised his eyes to the building, looking at it like it was a monster about to eat him alive. But he finally shuffled forward ahead of Tom and the preacher followed, remaining quiet for the moment. Inside, Loy stopped and studied the altar. Then he lifted his eyes to the cross beyond, glanced around the sanctuary to his left and right, and finally looked askance at the ceiling above, cringing as if expecting Heaven to rain down judgment.

"Let's go to my office." Tom gently steered Loy through the short hallway. He shifted the two chairs in front of his desk a little closer to each other and offered one to the older man.

Loy finally met Tom's eyes and his brow furrowed. Then he looked down at the chair several seconds before taking the seat, but he sat perched on the front edge, looking ready for flight any second.

Tom sat in the chair beside him instead of behind the desk. "How are you feeling today?"

Loy looked up, staring hard above Tom's head and to his right, not meeting his eyes this time. He shook his head almost imperceptibly, and in a near whisper uttered one word, "B-b-b-bad."

Tom sat back a few inches, and he couldn't resist looking over his shoulder as a chill spread through his body. He drew a deep breath and reached for the Bible on his desk. He opened the book to the Lord's Prayer and began to read aloud.

"Our father in heaven, hallowed be your name. Your kingdom come, your will be done on earth as it is in heaven."

Loy began to breathe heavy.

Tom stopped to look up at him. The man's face grew darker, and it set Tom's teeth on edge. Twisting his head to the right and thrusting his chin out at the same time, he literally snarled.

The preacher laid a hand on Loy's knee and spoke gently, "I'm just going to finish this reading and then we'll pray together. Then you can tell me about this creature and maybe I can help."

Loy straightened his neck and lowered his gaze for the moment.

Taking it as a sign to continue, Tom read on, but the heavy breathing returned, and the older man spit on the floor when the preacher read, "And do not lead us into temptation but deliver us from the evil one." As he finished the next line, "For yours is the kingdom and the power and the glory forever, Amen," Loy spit directly on the Bible and grabbed it from Tom's hands, throwing it across the room.

Then he jumped up to stand over Tom, snarling down at him. "You disgust me, little man. You think you have the courage to face me?" The words came out strong, clear and fast, with a voice, and a command of grammar, not Loy's own. At the same time, he stretched himself up taller than Tom would've thought possible and his body seemed to swell. The whites of his eyes filled with blood and the cornea appeared to glow red, the pupil still pitch black. "You ran and hid before. What makes you think you have the nerve to stand up to me now?"

Tom swallowed hard. The man before him still looked like Loy, mostly, but the creature was there in his eyes, his face, his voice. This wasn't Tom's meek, mentally disabled uncle speaking. "I'm not standing up to you on my own strength. And I'm not leaving this man to stand up to you alone either. I won't quit till he's free of you, and your kind."

The Loy who was not Loy pressed forward into Tom's face, now seemingly as tall as the preacher himself. No longer bent over and frail, his muscles stretched the baggy clothing to its limits. "I'll see you in hell first, preacher." The creature's arms swelled, its features contorting. "You think *He* doesn't know your sins, holy man?" The thing shifted its head upward when it spoke of God. "Holier than everyone else, aren't you, preacher? You come back here to this place to show them all the way, didn't you? Set them all straight. Especially that little red-headed nurse. Did your wife, Elizabeth, know she was coming to visit you, right here, in this holy place?"

Then while Loy's voice cried out in protest, the thing's face suddenly grimaced, registering pain. One hand slipped inside Loy's shirt to the waistband. As the bowie knife slid out of the tattered clothing, Tom froze, unable to get his limbs to move. But instead of attacking the preacher, the thing gritted its teeth and twisted its head to the side as the knife came down on its own wrist. And Loy screamed. From somewhere deep inside the massive creature, the frail old man screamed again and again. In a frenzy the creature that was also Loy upended the desk with one hand, crashing the computer and scattering papers all over the room.

Then the man's body spasmed and Loy seemed to shrink with the bowie knife still clutched in his fist. Blood dripping from his wrist, his face a crumpled mask, Loy finally appeared to take back control. And then he ran out, leaving the preacher quaking.

CHAPTER 23

Tuesday, November 23, 2010

While he was fleeing from the preacher, Loy's old four-wheeler ran out of gas, and he collapsed somewhere in the woods on his way back up the mountain. He woke the next day cold and confused, peeking an eye open to check the sky for the angle of the sun.

Early morning, he figured. His whole body ached. The blood had dried on the dirty rag he'd wrapped around his wrist. He uncurled from a fetal position and tried to stretch, but his muscles cramped, and the effort of standing made the woods around him pitch and roll. Water from a nearby stream braced him, only to have a wave of nausea drop him to his knees. He looked around to get his bearings, then scrambling to his feet, floundered off toward the old Hadley cabin.

He might even build a small fire to warm his bones. He had supplies enough stashed there, and he didn't think Miss Laurie would come back to that place anymore. Not since he nearly hurt her the last time.

Well, he'd warned her off at least.

Wasn't sure how, but he hoped for a chance to tell her how sorry he was. He'd been tryin' to watch out for her since she was a baby. Wasn't no problem when she lived far away, but now he'd failed. Glen only ever wanted her protected from the evil him and Curry had brought on the family, and he'd set Loy to the task. Well, Loy had tried, but Curry and that beast had bucked him at every turn.

"Don't you ever let her be taken again. You hear me? Swear it. Swear it now. On your life." Glen had got up in Loy's face. *"You*

do whatever you have to do." He'd pointed at the hunting rifle in Loy's hands. *"She'd be better off dead, you hear me, boy?"* Glen's face got red and the spit flew, but Loy nodded hard. He knew exactly what his brother wanted. And now, all these years later, he knew what it meant for him too. If he had to die to save her, then that's what he'd do.

The cabin appeared in the trees. He'd hole up there for a few hours, get some rest. Best of all, it wasn't far from Momma's. He wanted to see her one more time, too. Tell her he loved her, and he never meant no harm to nobody.

The sun had gotten a mite higher in the sky by the time he sat down to eat a slice of bread and a piece of cheese. He heated a pot of coffee over the fire and browned the leftover half of a hot dog. The food he kept in a battered red and white Igloo chest outside under the porch, the nearly empty coffee can he'd tucked in a corner of one of the cupboards, using just enough at a time to make a light brown watery brew.

His gnawing belly sated, his body warmed, he laid down on the floor and, with a smudged and shaking hand, pulled a threadbare blanket over his bony shoulder. The beast inside him went quiet... for now. It wouldn't stay that way, he knew. It was almost time. Hopefully he'd get the chance to see his momma. Say goodbye. Find Miss Laurie again, try to keep his promise.

CHAPTER 24

Wednesday, November 24, 2010

Organizing a man-beast hunt proved more time consuming than Blaine planned. He'd had to rearrange duties among the deputies, pull Adam off a regular assignment, and gather what to some might appear an inordinate amount of fire power, including dart guns and tranquilizers. He was trying to keep this thing as quiet as possible, not get people talking too much, but it wasn't easy.

When he called Ashe County Wild Animal Control, he told them they were having difficulty with a large, aggressive animal hanging around too close to homes, scaring people, insinuating it might need to be put down. Though it felt less than honest to mislead the man, if the guy thought he meant a black bear, well, that couldn't be helped. Animal Control would have to send one of their own men, Blaine knew that, but he hoped they wouldn't feel the need to call out an army. It wasn't the first time they'd dealt with wildlife issues in the area. Of course, they would want to capture and relocate the animal if it could be deemed safe to do so. He wondered where Animal Control might designate a safe enough place to re-home a demon-wolf.

Problem was, Blaine still wasn't sure exactly what they were dealing with. He'd fought the creature hand to hand, and yet he couldn't decide if it was real, or his own vivid imagination, or some trick of the mind. And he didn't want to kill Loy if he didn't have to. His badge didn't make him a law unto himself, despite his suspicions about the man's involvement in Lilly's death. But if he ran into that *thing...* he wanted to be prepared either way.

Blaine intended to get out early to see Laura before he set off into Porter's Hollow in search of Loy. He needed to reassure himself she was safe. But more than that, he wanted to make sure she didn't go out looking for her uncle on her own. And he wanted to find out where her final loyalties would lay. If it came down to it, would she interfere with his duty to bring Loy in, and would she hold it against him if it meant the man's death?

With orders issued, his gear packed up in the SUV, and Duke seated shotgun, he finally headed out to the Perkins' place around 10:00 A.M. Less than twenty minutes later he turned onto the farm lane to find Laura scuffing along in hiking boots, head down. She stopped and turned toward him as he slowed, and his heart did a stomach dive.

He ordered Duke into the back seat as he pulled alongside her and popped the passenger door open. "Give you a lift?" Aware he was interrupting her walk, and her contemplations, he added, "If you don't mind."

Her fresh showered scent wafted in ahead of her. Laura settled into the spot vacated by the dog and she spoke to the animal first. "You didn't have to move on my account." She reached up to pet the eager mutt who had positioned his front feet on the console and pushed his head between them to offer a greeting.

Blaine considered them both for a moment. Animals had a sixth sense, there was no doubt. Stories of dogs rescuing their human companions before anyone else knew they were in danger, sniffing out oncoming illness, even warding off impending disaster, filled the accounts of animal behaviorists. But that was usually for their own handler. Duke had shown an odd attachment to Laura from the moment he'd met her, as if he'd been appointed her sentinel. For some reason the notion chilled Blaine to the core, even as it warmed his heart to know the dog loved her as much as he did. And she definitely loved Duke.

"He's been whining at me a lot lately. I think he misses being with you."

She smiled without taking her eyes off the dog. That smile. That soft, sweet, gentle, woman smile. His insides had a meltdown. But it was time to get real. He had to be tough, make sure she understood this time. Pulling up under the overhanging branches of the old shagbark hickory, Blaine shut the car off and turned toward Laura, ready to tackle the situation, but she interrupted him.

"I was going to call you. I need to go see Tom and Elizabeth today, so I won't be home for a while. We've still got Thanksgiving dinner to plan, and it's tomorrow." She stopped and looked up at him. "Cayley will be with Aunt Hattie and I'll check in with her from time to time. I'll be back later this evening, but I'll have my phone with me if you need to be in touch. Please keep me updated about the search for Loy."

Whoosh! Just like that, she disarmed him like a skilled veteran. He'd been all set to lecture her on not getting involved in the search and she'd whipped the rug right out from under him, leaving him fumbling for his next words.

"Yeah, sure." He struggled to remember what he'd gotten so worked up about. "Sounds like a good idea." Why had he been so worried? "Being with family—at a time like this, I mean." His best arguments against the impulsive recklessness of rushing into things she was unqualified and ill-prepared for went up in a puff.

Laura asked, "You will have your cell phone on you, right?"

He laid a hand on his belt case and nodded. Then he started to open the car door, but sudden suspicion drew him back. "You will stay off the mountain and out of the woods then?" He looked her in the eye.

"I have no plans of going out into those woods alone again. Not as long as that... *thing*... roams free. I assure you."

CHAPTER 25

Upstairs in her bedroom, Laura readied herself the best she could. Tom had called to share the chilling details of his encounter with Loy at the church the day before. They'd decided between them to go to Beulah's and see if she could get Loy to come back again. If Beulah rang the dinner bell, Loy wouldn't ignore it in case his momma needed him. Then they would try to lure him into the garage shed that had been a sort of sanctuary for Loy and his brothers.

Technically then, Laura hadn't lied to Blaine. She wasn't planning on going into the woods after him, and she wouldn't be alone.

She drew her knife out of its holster. Not so much a hunting knife as a hiker's tool, it was a fixed blade survival knife meant for roughing it in the woods. But it had slowed the creature down before and she'd have to leave the shotgun behind with Cayley for protection. The girl had grit. Laura knew she could trust her to watch out for Aunt Hattie, but the odd connection between Cayley and Tom was still unsettling.

Sure, he'd skipped town when he was young to avoid family curses and demons, and she could hardly criticize him for it, but his character had otherwise proved unblemished, at least as far as she knew. And there were far too many years between the two in age for anything to have happened between them—physically— weren't there? Any connection had to have come in the years since Tom's return to the hollow, married and licensed as a preacher. Still, Laura couldn't rid herself of the gut feeling her brother and the CNA were bound by unseen ties—ties she worried could be his downfall.

Shaking off the sensation, she grabbed her cell phone and headed downstairs, stopping just long enough to say goodbye to Aunt Hattie. Then she climbed into the Toyota, hoping everyone she loved would survive this day.

Tom had tried to contact the old priest once more, but there had been no answer. So, it looked like they might only have each other to depend on. Well, sort of. If her brother was right, they weren't really alone in this—not if the almighty genuinely cared about simple, ordinary people like Loy. True, Tom was a preacher, so maybe he *had* to claim belief in a greater power personally concerned for human welfare. But with him, it didn't seem like just words. It was in his eyes, in the way he talked to people, in his gentle, non-judgmental way. For him, it was all so real. She only hoped this wouldn't be the undoing of that humble, innocent faith.

Arriving at the preacher's house, Laura pulled up behind a black, older model Chevy Impala. Still in the driver's seat, a large man checked his rearview mirror and stared at her, shifting it with one hand, squinting. She hoped her brother wasn't getting company he'd have to entertain. There was so much at stake, so much depending on what they did this day.

The man in the Chevy opened his door and pulled himself out of the car by the roof frame. Laura shut the Toyota off, causing the aged and sizeable gentleman to turn and peer at her above a pair of gold, thin-rimmed glasses. He wasn't fat so much as, well the most apt word seemed *big*... the kind legends would call a giant of a man. Everything about him appeared oversized. With huge, meaty hands, and thick arms and body, he was taller than Laura by a foot. Looking up, she realized the big man wore a simple black suit with a white cleric's collar. *The priest?*

Tom chose that moment to step out onto the porch. Staring hard at the other man, his face registered surprise and he came rushing out to meet them.

"Father Gahlen." Tom slapped a hand on the priest's shoulder, literally turning the fellow around to face him and grabbing one of those big paws in a solid grip. Though tall himself, Tom wasn't quite eye to eye with the cleric, and not nearly the size and bulk of the other man. Still, he pulled the priest into a powerful hug before the older man could react.

"This is my sister Laura," he said turning toward her, hand still gripping the priest's shoulder. "Laura, this is Father Gahlen Doherty. Father, I can't tell you how relieved I am to see you. I prayed you'd come. You'll stay here of course. I'll set you up with a room, but you've showed up just in the nick of time." He nodded toward Laura to follow.

"Then you haven't confronted him yet?" The priest's deep, calm voice resonated with concern, but he stayed put.

Tom stopped, dropping his gaze to his feet. "Actually, I have. Once." When he looked up the priest's face had turned a shade paler. "He wrecked the church office and ran. Disappeared into the woods."

"Did it, I mean did *he*, know things?" The priest drilled Tom with a stare. "Things you would find—difficult—or uncomfortable having exposed before others? Is there anything in either of your pasts?"

He turned that look on Laura. She stayed silent.

"It will use everything your uncle might know about anyone and anything it can do to distract or disable you. It will not be kind. It will not preserve anyone's dignity or pride. It will invent things, lies."

Father Gahlen raised a finger at them.

"It will make your best intentions sound like lewd, sadistic schemes. It will seem to know things about me it can't possibly know. *And*, it will take its turn with anyone present. This will be the ugliest, most frightening confrontation—the most sinister battle—you've ever faced. You won't be able to tell the difference between its truth and its lies. You'll likely doubt each other as a result. You will be inclined to doubt me, and your uncle may not survive." He glanced from one to the other, his face doleful, his shoulders drooping. "And none of you will ever be the same."

Laura watched her brother's reaction intently. Tom's head hung down and his lips moved silently several seconds before he looked up to answer. "I'm no holier than the next man. I know that, but I intend to help my uncle and rid the hollow of that thing. I'm not backing out now."

The priest's jaw muscle flexed as he stared at Laura. She knew he was expecting a response; they both were. Her mouth had gone dry and she found it hard to breathe, till she suddenly took in a deep gulp of air and blew it out hard. Eyes wide, she nodded, but words wouldn't come, so she simply followed the men into the house to lay their plans.

CHAPTER 26

The search began at Hattie Perkins' place. Sheriff Wilson set out with Duke in the lead, followed by Adam Richardson and two more deputies, the most he could draw away from other duties and not raise undue attention. The Animal Control officer brought up the rear as the group searched for Loy's four-day old trail. Their best hope was to pick up on a new one, though Blaine realized that would mean Loy had recently lingered near Hattie's in hopes of catching Laura alone and off-guard. The idea the old man clung to her for some reason made Blaine's gut churn.

After using a shirt he'd taken from Loy's room for scent, Blaine started Duke across the field. The dog picked up the smell within a hundred yards of the old tobacco shed, along the wood's edge beside a large upright tree stump. The sheriff pictured the creature hunched there watching Laura, and a dark rage surged through his veins. That this thing could actually be some sort of demon... Blaine couldn't give in to the idea.

No matter what he'd seen, or thought he'd seen, he wasn't convinced. More likely Loy and his brothers had concocted the idea long ago to attempt to lay their blame on anything else. These were men, just ordinary men, bent on notorious evil. The thought spurred him, and he raced ahead of the others with Duke, determined to put an end to these psycho games.

The trail kept leading up into the mountain in much the same direction they'd found the caves before. A chilling thought began to take over—the image of Laura, bloody and battered. Interrupting his thoughts, Duke suddenly stopped. He circled several times, raised his nose to the air and bobbed his head. Then, muzzle pointed southwest toward the hollow, he stood staring several seconds. At last, Duke lowered his nose to the ground and made for the caves once more, but he slowed significantly, stopping every few hundred yards to sniff the air. If the dog registered this much confusion, it probably meant the man had been all over the area, most likely in the last twenty-four hours. It could prove difficult to narrow down his location.

Duke stopped again, ears pitched toward some unseen threat or discovery. Seconds later, a low snuffling growl reached Blaine's ears. He quickly attached the dog's leash and held it short, signaling Duke to move ahead, quietly advancing as the snuffling continued. Too late, the sheriff realized they were upwind of whatever was making the noise.

The element of surprise already gone, he encouraged Duke forward faster. Seconds later the dog charged into a bramble of fallen trees covered in vines and one very large black bear charged out the other side, lumbering away. Blaine was unaware of any bears that big in the local area. He was almost drawn to follow it, but they couldn't afford the time lost. For Duke's part, he was young and his lack of experience accounted for his reaction. He set off, dragging Blaine after the beast, forgetting he was supposed to be on the scent he'd been given.

But jumping over a dead log, Duke suddenly stopped and circled. He dug his nose into something in the leaves, giving the sheriff time to gain control again. Blaine was sure the mutt had most likely uncovered bear scat and stopped to investigate, but what he nudged with the toe of his boot turned out to be an old rag of some kind. He grabbed a stick and lifted the soiled, once white cloth. Dried blood, but not long dried. It was still dark cherry black in the center, a lighter reddish hue around the edges. *Wounded?* And it couldn't have been more than a few hours ago. Blaine glanced around. His crew was probably nearly a mile behind.

Duke sat down—his sign he'd found what he was supposed to be searching for—but the dog could be forgiven his confusion. The sheriff pulled Loy's shirt out of the bag he'd sealed it in and put it in front of the animal's nose. Duke indicated the other cloth again.

Blaine rewarded the dog with a treat since both pieces held traces of Loy's scent, though they'd have to start over. Duke didn't yet understand his task completely. They needed to find the man himself, not more traces of him. But in the next instant, the dog lifted his muzzle to the air, then started off again, turning completely away from the caves, and heading southeast back down the mountain toward Porter's Hollow. Blaine decided to trust the animal's nose. He managed to radio Adam as he ripped through the underbrush with Duke still on the leash.

When they topped the ridge above the old Hadley cabin, the sheriff realized where they were heading. It was still out of sight and some distance below, but he knew they'd have to go check it out. He wished he'd thought to do that first and saved all this time rambling through the trees. But the man hid better in the woods and mountains than any wild animal. Better even than his brother. While Curry had been like a mountain lion, hiding and stalking, Loy was more like a weasel, scurrying, scrambling and secreting away in every conceivable hole or burrow.

By now the team would have found the site where Duke changed direction and be checking out the trail beyond. Adam would be thorough, so if Blaine had missed anything by letting Duke turn and have his own head, the deputy would pick it up. But they'd lose time up there, and he'd be on his own if he came on Loy in the cabin. He shrugged off the persistent feeling something was terribly wrong even now as the old place came into view.

Duke's head popped up and he stood stock still, testing the air. Then he tugged so hard on the lead, Blaine nearly fell forward. He caught his balance on the run and the dog charged for the cabin, but the sheriff didn't want to burst in guns blazing. He finally managed to pull up on the leash and rein the dog in about a hundred yards out, placing his hand on Duke's head, silently ordering him to sit. Blaine stood behind a tree and waited. Nothing stirred. No smoke from the teetering chimney, no sign of life, human or... the radio crackled, and he didn't finish the thought.

"Tracks leading ... caves look old." Static overran Adam's voice, and the sheriff heard, "... guess is ... ones you're following ... fresher. What ... want us... do, Sheriff? Over."

Blaine frowned at the handset. The noise echoed around the woods, startling nearby birds. He cringed and butted the radio with the heel of one hand. These military grade things were usually much better than this up here in the mountains. The weather didn't even disrupt them in his experience, and today was a calm, barely cloudy fall day.

As quiet but clear as he could, he replied, "Send Bud and Troy to check out the caves. Tell them to set up watch there for now and report back every half hour till they hear from one of us. You bring Animal Control and follow my trail."

Silence lingered several minutes, then he heard, "The guy wants ... how big this ... we're chasin'. He ... signs of ... and prints headin' ... direction. Wants ... check ... out. Don't know ... going on. Or ... exactly what ... lookin' for. Just sayin'. Over."

"No. Follow my trail. No time to argue. Head toward the Hadley cabin. Keep the chatter down and just get moving," Blaine answered.

Again, the radio was quiet several seconds. "Roger ... our way ... few minutes. Over ... out."

The sheriff drew a deep breath and picked his way through the woods to the cabin. Adam wouldn't be far behind. But already he suspected the stillness here was real. Duke's nose and ears were alert and yet the dog was calm. He led Blaine right up to the cabin door, which stood only slightly ajar. Blaine checked the windows. Nothing moved, and Duke simply sat down on the porch, nose pointing at the door.

The sheriff pulled up on the handle, lifting the weight of the wood so it wouldn't scrape as he opened it. Still it creaked, a lonely, eerie sound in the quiet that had grown since he stood watching from above. He cocked his head and listened.

Silence.

Duke lifted his nose and bobbed his head again. The odor of sweat and stale coffee met the sheriff's nose, and yet another scent. Burnt ash. He crossed the room and held a hand over the fireplace. Faint warmth emanated from its cinders.

He checked out the rest of the cabin, but there was no other trace of man... or beast. Then he headed outside, circling the place, checking for tracks when Duke's nose went to the ground. The dog dug in the brush and debris near the corner of the cabin and sniffed out an old Igloo cooler under the porch, then turned and headed away from the steps into the woods again and pulled on the lead.

Several yards out Duke suddenly went wild barking, digging, circling a single spot, frantic with eagerness. The sheriff pulled him close and made him sit. The dog had uncovered a large rock with bits of cloth stuck to it, a pale blue denim of the kind Laura often wore—partially stained with dried blood.

When Blaine let Duke move on, the dog took off at a frenzied pace. They headed north for several hundred yards, coming close to retracing their path down the mountain, causing the sheriff to think they were coming full circle back to Hattie's. But the dog suddenly turned sharply across the grade, traveling parallel to the hollow below. This direction would lead them to the trail above Beulah Porter's home maybe another mile or so further.

Judging by Duke's reaction to the scent trail, either Loy must've headed home again recently, or the dog had honed-in on Laura somewhere not far off, and she was quite possibly in imminent danger—*or maybe both.*

He tried to raise Adam on the handset but there was no answer, and no time to wait. They set off at a clip, Duke pulling persistently on the lead. Laura had said she'd be at Tom's but...? Despite the tug and pull of the dog and the rush of the moment, Blaine's heart ached, his stomach plummeting at the thought of possibly losing her forever.

CHAPTER 27

The old priest kept repeating prayers in Latin all the way to Beulah's. Laura watched him finger the cross around his neck with one hand, clutching a black leather Bible in the other, his voice a monotone as he chanted the same set of words over and over.

Tom sighed deep before shoving the gear shift into park when they pulled up in front of the white, weathered clapboard. He turned to Laura in the back seat, their eyes meeting in a long look of dread, fear, sorrow. Neither one was prepared, but both were determined to follow through with the plan.

"Ready?" he said, shifting his gaze to the priest.

The older man went silent, staring straight ahead out the window, his fingers falling away from the cross.

At last the priest replied, "Can a person be ready to enter the gates of hell?" Father Gahlen rubbed his face roughly. "There is no such thing as being ready..." He let his words trail off and grabbed the door handle.

All three trudged up the porch steps, but Tom took the lead and knocked firmly on Beulah's door. Laura stared up at the iron triangle her grandmother used to call Loy, but the striker no longer hung on the post.

Then came the familiar shuffling noise. "Who's bangin' at my door now?" the old woman called out.

"It's me, Granny, Tom. I'm here with Laurie Allen and a friend of ours. Could we talk with you a minute?"

The silence lingered, until finally the lock clicked and the door opened a narrow space. The old woman, staying back out of sight, spoke again. "Been an awful lotta talk goin' on lately. Not sure I'm in the mood for it."

"We're sorry, Granny, but it's really important. It's about Loy. We know he's been hurting himself. We just want to help him." Laura stepped forward as she spoke, and Beulah peeked her head around the door.

Seconds passed while the elderly woman stared blindly at Laura, but at last she stepped back, allowing them to pass through single file, though it proved to be a tight squeeze for the big priest. When they turned to face her, Beulah honed in on the cleric, fixing him with a hard, mistrustful look, pinning him in place.

"Well," the old woman finally turned her face to Laura with that unseeing, omniscient gaze. "Who's this fella? An' what business he got comin' here?"

"I'm sorry, Granny, this is..." Laura hesitated. Should she tell her grandmother, a staunch old-fashioned Baptist, that they'd brought a Catholic priest into her home to help her son? She could introduce him by name only. Tell the other woman he was just a friend. Laura glanced at her brother. His eyebrows rose and he shrugged. So, the staunch Baptist preacher was capable of deception if the situation compelled.

No, enough already. It was time she faced life head on. "This is Father Gahlen Doherty. He's come out here from Illinois to help us figure out this thing that's been tormenting Loy, and the rest of our family."

Beulah took a step back, appearing to consider the idea. "Can' say as I'd call any man *Father* that a way, but..." she pursed her lips, her head nodding slow, "...reckon the almighty's big enough to listen to them what calls on him. No matter what they call themselves."

Laura let out a breath, not aware she'd been holding it in till her grandmother started toward the kitchen.

"C'mon through then." Granny gestured toward the room ahead.

Directly behind the elderly woman and in front of the men, Laura noticed something she'd missed. Clutched in her grandmother's left hand, hanging down by her side and partially obscured by the folds of her apron, she held the long, slim, iron striker.

CHAPTER 28

Sitting bolt upright, Loy swiveled his head in every direction, trying to take in all the dark corners of the cabin. Something woke him, but what? He tried to think, but the pain, "Ah!"

He cringed.

Grabbing his aching head in both hands, he bent forward toward his drawn-up knees. His eyes focused on his bare feet, poking out below filthy pant legs. They were just as dirty. And they were cold, so cold. He tried to concentrate on the icy sensation. Maybe if he kept his blood and body chilled, he could freeze the creature out.

Clang, clang, clang.

The sound. That's what woke him, not the beast.

Clang, clang. Then another long pause and it started again. *Clang, clang, clang.*

Momma was calling.

Scrabbling to put on his boots, Loy grabbed his hat and ran for the four-wheeler, clutching at the bowie knife in his belt.

CHAPTER 29

Stopping briefly in the kitchen, Laura turned and reached for Tom's arm, nodding toward the striker in their grandmother's hand. Eyes wide, she searched his face. They watched as the old woman sat down behind the table. Father Gahlen gave them a quizzical look.

"Granny," Tom prompted, "is Loy here?"

Beulah lifted her chin, turning her face in his direction. "Not yet." She lowered her head, fixing her blind eyes at a spot somewhere to his left.

Tom shifted his own gaze to Laura and the priest in turn. "We need to talk with him. Soon as possible. You think he'll be here soon?"

The elderly woman sighed. Dropping her chin to her chest, she got quiet, and a tear rolled down her withered cheek.

Laura could stand it no longer. She sat down next to her grandmother and put her arm around the woman's sagging shoulders. "Granny, we really just want to help, before he does himself serious harm." *And preferably before the sheriff takes him off to jail.* Laura kept this thought to herself, but it fueled her urgency. "We can't help him if we can't find him."

The woman's head stayed low for several long seconds, and she sat without making a sound, head cocked slightly. Then passing right outside, the rumble of the old beat up four-wheeler broke the silence and she turned her face to Tom. "That'd be him."

The three conspirators glanced at each other. Laura stood slowly while the old woman remained seated, not offering to move. Only then did Laura notice the bag and shotgun on the floor. Granny Beulah must've sensed Laura's thoughts.

The elderly woman stood and grabbed Laura's arm. "I rang the bell to git 'im here one last time. So's I could send him away with jus' what he could carry—for good." Her jaw flexed and she pointed a crooked finger at her granddaughter, and then at the other two, one at a time. "You hurt him, you'll have more than that thing to deal with. I ain't no stranger to conjurin' m'self." She leveled her gleaming milky blind eyes at each one in turn in that disconcerting way she had, making you feel like she could see right into your soul.

Mouth open, eyes wide, Laura turned to her brother. His brow creased even as his eyes widened, apparently at the same loss for words. The woman had never let on. She'd said her husband wouldn't have anything to do with such things, but she'd never claimed the same about her own involvement. Laura hadn't asked. She never thought to raise the question—or so much as entertain the thought. Not with her own grandmother.

"He's pullin' up," Beulah said. "I ain't goin' to draw him in for ya." She turned away. "You explain it to him. What you plan to do," she added as she headed for the living room.

Shock rippled through the group as they eyed each other. Laura shook her head slowly, the big priest rubbed his sweating brow, and Tom shrugged his shoulders. He was the first to move, reaching for the back door handle even as the four-wheeler went silent. When Father Gahlen followed, Laura finally found her feet again, woodenly putting one in front of the other in a daze.

Tom slowly leaned through the doorway. Then he turned and, raising a finger near his lips, he mouthed, *"In the shed."* They wouldn't even have to lead him into their trap. The man had gone straight there on his own. Or was he leading them?

The thought made Laura's heart skip a beat, but stepping out onto the back stoop Tom moved stealthily, turning and waving for Laura and the priest to follow.

The cool, damp air sent a chill through Laura and she swallowed hard. Trying to take a silent deep breath she wondered, *Oh, God, what have we gotten ourselves into?* Outside the sky had darkened, the woods had gone silent. The breeze stilled. Nothing chattered. Nothing moved.

Until they neared the shed.

A barred owl hooted three times, then swooped down across the space in front of them into a treetop beyond. Beside the tree stood the wraithlike figure of a young woman—the one Laura now knew was Blaine's dead wife. Anger, accusation and something else in her face. Longing, hope, fear? But before Laura could react, a loud scraping drew her attention. The shed door. Loy had appeared in the opening. His clothes were dirty and tattered. His shoulders drooped and his face was pained, agony written in every fold and smudge.

"Ain't—goin'—wi'—you," he stumbled over the words, aiming the remark at Tom.

"We don't mean to take you anywhere. We just want to have a talk with you. See if we can't help you do something about those." Tom nodded his head at Loy's arms. "You don't have to hurt yourself if you let us help you."

Loy looked askance at Tom and then the big priest. Then his eyes came to rest on Laura.

"Please let us come in and talk with you," Laura pleaded. "I won't let anyone hurt you. You've always watched out for me, haven't you?"

Loy cast his gaze on the ground a moment, then lifted his chin to look Laura in the eye. Nodding his head slow, his face looked even sadder.

"Can't—l-l-let—him—hurt—L-L-Laurie. No m-m-matter—wh-wh-what." Loy's head dipped with each stutter, clearly struggling to form the words.

Laura stepped forward from between Tom and Father Gahlen, reaching for her uncle's hand. His fingers cold, muscles limp, she took it in both of hers, sharing her warmth. He raised his eyes to hers once more, the battle in his mind behind those pinpoint black pupils painfully obvious. Before she realized what was happening, Loy yanked her back into the shed with more force than she thought possible, slamming the rickety door, and slapping a wooden bar down across the braces.

Eyes adjusting to the dim light inside the building, Laura looked into the twisted face of the man gripping her arm. Aware of a pinching pain in her bicep, she flinched, and the creature's voice assaulted her.

"You afraid, little girl?" he snarled. "You should be. We've got you now. You won't get away so easy this time." He bent his face to hers and the corneas of his eyes began to glow. She gasped for air as he drew her into his chest, staring down at her. Then suddenly the fire began to dull. The glow ebbed and Loy's ragged features warped into a grimace. His grip on her arm loosened, his body sagged, but he didn't move.

Trembling and still struggling to breathe, Laura somehow reacted. Instantaneously, she peeled away from his hold and scrambled for the wooden bar he'd dropped across the door. It shifted upwards but stuck by a few inches on the metal support, and she screamed when Loy grabbed her from behind. Then the door burst open with a bang as Tom exploded through, Father Gahlen on his heels.

The preacher lunged for Loy, and the big priest grabbed Laura.

"Lock the door. Hurry," Tom yelled as he pushed Loy backwards.

Father Gahlen reached for the bar, dragging Laura with him. Then he turned, raising the cross around his neck before him, and began to chant. "*In nomine Patris et Filii et Spiritus Sancti...*" The Latin words that followed were unintelligible to Laura. Loy shrank visibly, shaking his head, staring up at Tom, whose own lips were moving in a less audible prayer.

She looked around wildly for another exit, just in case. The men so focused on their plan to exorcise the demon, they wouldn't likely plan for the need to escape in the event they failed. She quickly discovered a side door near the back, padlocked from the inside.

She scanned the rest of the one-room shed in a desperate glance. No windows, but light streamed through the cracks in the wood siding, intensifying the dimness around her, making it hard for Laura to see her uncle's face.

She stepped forward, and the change in him was immediate. His expression hardened. His eyes glittered in a beam of light and they began to glow. He doubled over, his whole appearance darkening. When he straightened up again, the creature that was still Loy but continued to change, shrugged off the preacher's grip, though in truth the man may have simply relaxed it in shock.

Those eyes bored into the preacher as the thing spoke with Loy's voice, but clear and strong without his stuttering hesitation. "Go ahead. Pray all you want. God won't help you here. This isn't holy ground. This place, this hollow, this mountain, even the very soil here belongs to *him*. *We* gave it to him a long time ago." The beast spoke to Tom but turned its eyes on the cleric briefly, while the priest did exactly that, praying continuously, raising the gold cross, making the sign of the crucifix in front of the creature.

Continuing on in English now, in a voice steady and strong, Father Gahlen prayed like he knew the one he was talking to intimately, and as if no one else were present.

The creature sneered at the priest and focused on Tom again, its voice changed. Deeper, hard-edged, gloating, its pronouns changing from *we*, and *him*... "*You* for instance, gave me time to establish myself here."

Its leering gaze slid over Laura next. "And you. You played your part. '*Ahhh, Mommy, it's the wolf man, he's coming again!*' Your baby cries got you out of town and left me all the time in the world to work. Not to mention freeing up your father's time for me." The sneer grew, and he rose taller, glaring at her. "And it was oh so easy for you to push it all away and leave everyone to their own defenses, wasn't it? Your granny, your daddy, your poor retarded uncle. You just went on living your own life, far away from them all—safe and happy."

Laura had trouble connecting the voice with a man as simple as Loy Porter. Then he turned his head, adjusting his gaze to find her eyes. "All those young, tender beauties. Your Uncle Curry savored every one. He thought of you with every touch. Every panting breath. Every small frightened whimper. Every sad, tearful plea for mercy. And especially every glittering, innocent pair of eyes."

Laura covered her ears, dropping her head, shaking. The creature's voice created an evil grating din in her brain. Its very breath nearly made her swoon. And she wasn't a woman who ever swooned. But her stomach roiled, and her face burned. Yet all of it came from the innocent look of her Uncle Loy, mentally disabled, physically battered, and psychologically torn apart.

Suddenly, Father Gahlen's strong voice rose loud and demanding. "What is your name?" he commanded.

The thing inside her uncle turned its leering gaze on the big priest. It tilted its head to one side and then the other, considering the cleric as if it just remembered he was there. It reared back and growled low, then it shook its head slowly, wagging one long, thin, clawed finger. "Ah, ah, ah. Our name is ours to command, not yours, old man."

The creature's body swelled, stretching the flimsy rags Loy wore, but the demon-wolf was still held in check for now. Whether by Loy's will, or by the priest's power, or by the thing's own choice, Laura couldn't tell.

Now the creature leaned forward, leveling its eyes with Father Gahlen's. "We know you. You have no authority here. You got that girl killed didn't you, holy man? Her and the innocent little demon growing inside her." It drew back and stretched up before it added, "But not before you took her? Plunged yourself into her sweet white body, didn't you, priest? All those visits with her alone. Did you really think no one would suspect, simply because you were a priest?"

Despite her determination not to believe the creature or be lured in by anything it said, Laura made a small, sharp exclamation of shock. The ghastly image it described seeped into her mind as it spoke, running vividly in her conscious like a terrible, frightening horror movie. She drew back.

Even Tom paused in his quiet prayer and sucked in a breath as if he'd been punched in the stomach. His head came up and his face went white.

Father Gahlen didn't miss a beat. He raised his hand, making the sign of the cross with the gold crucifix grasped between his finger and thumb, and continued, "We command you in the name of the Father, and of the Son, and of the Holy Spirit."

The creature appeared to shrink, almost imperceptibly.

Turning in angry frustration on Tom it spat out, "Preacher?" As if the word was a joke. "Your sister, your friends, do they know what you really are—Baby Killer?"

Tom's shoulders fell and his face crumpled, all attempt at prayer apparently forgotten. Loy's sneer turned to a look of pure evil pleasure at having gotten the best of his opponent. The small, seeming innocence of the man with the leering unearthly voice created a more frightening, sinister effect somehow than if the thing had appeared at its unholy worst. *That* you could hate outright, *that* you could fear with good reason. This amalgam of the simple, gentle man and the horrendous evil demon had left Laura, and from the looks of it, Tom, completely abashed.

The priest, however, had so far held his own.

The thing continued to sneer at Tom. "Never told them how you fixed that girl up with an old woman and her coat hooks, did you, preacher? And whose baby was that one, holy man?"

Then its eyes slid from Tom to Laura, coming back to focus on the priest with a smirk. The beast inside Loy squared up with the old cleric, sizing him up like a boxer in a ring, looking for any weak points to exploit. Then its gaze shifted toward the thin wooden door and the two-by-four barring it shut. But the self-assured sneer lifting its lips melted away as a new sound reached the inside of the rickety shed.

Checking the faces around the room, Laura realized it must have dawned on them all at once—the barking, the voice calling out, all coming closer with a rush. Seconds later, something slammed into the door with a force that splintered several boards. The scratching, scraping, and pounding that followed grew in volume and force until one plank broke through and Duke's snout appeared in the opening. He snarled and growled and barked ferociously.

Then came the unmistakable voice of Blaine Wilson. "Come out, now," he yelled. "Come out and I'll call off the dog."

Suddenly everything went silent. The air in the shed was thick, tense, volatile. Like an electric current, it ran through Laura's body. The hair on her arms stood up and she squeezed both fists tight. Her eyes grew wide and her head raised till her gaze met her uncle's, one second before he launched.

Door boards cracked and splintered, light rushed through the opening and the mixed blur of white teeth and dark fur that burst through growled like a wild animal. That, and two other things registered in Laura's conscious mind before she blacked out. Her ribs were compressed so hard she could barely breathe, and her body had been jerked backward, feet dragging.

CHAPTER 30

Chaos reigned inside the little shed. Blaine caught a glimpse of Laura being dragged through a busted side door as Tom sprang into action chasing after her and Loy Porter. A giant of an elderly man in priest's garb stood holding a gold cross high, praying aloud in what sounded like a mix of English and Latin, and Duke charged after the group disappearing ahead.

The sheriff wasted no time trying to figure it all out. He broke through the debris and dashed after Laura, even as the big priest followed on his heels, his praying silenced.

Duke had bolted past Tom and reached Loy, circling around him, weighing the situation only briefly before he lunged, ramming hard into the back of the man's legs, teeth seeking purchase. Laura hung from Loy's arms, limp, apparently unconscious, but seemingly unharmed.

Blaine sprang past Tom, ready to go into action. Service revolver pulled, he circled behind the dog.

The Baptist preacher stood in front of the small group with both hands up, pleading loudly, "Let her go. She isn't the one you want. You need me. I'm the next male Porter in line. I have what you want. The strength, the stain, the curse is on me and the men in our family." His eyes found Blaine's and he shouted, "Call the dog off. She'll get hurt."

Thinking quick on his feet, the sheriff decided Tom was right. If they wanted to get Laura away from her crazed uncle safely, he'd have to back the dog off. He only hoped the animal would read the urgency in his voice and obey in time. He lowered the revolver but still holding it firmly in one hand shouted, "Duke, *stop!*"

The dog had fought hard to attach a biting grip on the back of Loy's upper thigh. He growled and pulled, resisting the command.

Blaine rushed forward, daring to get in close. He grabbed the dog's collar, and pulling hard, he commanded again, "Duke. *Stop! Down.*" He bit off the words hard and sharp. The sheriff felt the instant the release came and immediately ordered loud and firm, "Sit." Duke obeyed this time, though his hackles stood on a razor's edge. The sudden shift in Loy's weight caused the man to stagger and fall sideways, taking Laura down with him, grip still solidly around her middle.

That's when the big priest stepped around Tom, lifting the cross again, closing in on Loy. His voice raised in Latin supplication, unfamiliar to Blaine, his face solemn, fearless, angry. He stood directly over the creature in Loy's body, commanding it to release the woman and face him as God's messenger.

The evil being that was still recognizable as Loy, rose to its feet, pulling Laura up with it, backing away from the cleric, while she regained consciousness, shaking her head, wide eyes pleading. And the only force holding the thing back came from the biggest, burliest priest Blaine had ever seen.

CHAPTER 31

The creature that was in Loy, using the weak, frail man, grew taller. Its muscles swelled. Its shoulders spread. Keeping one thick, coarse-haired arm wrapped around Laura, the creature leaned its head down and growled, "Your daddy would be ashamed of you, Laurie Allen. His little girl just never was brave enough to face anything on her own." Its vile lips against Laura's ear, it continued, "It's your fault, you know. All of it." Its foul breath choking her, it gave a nod toward Blaine. "You could have saved the sheriff's pretty little wife. But it's okay, you can comfort him now, can't you? It's what you've wanted since you met him, isn't it? To open your legs... ooh, I'm sorry... your heart, to the big, strong, handsome sheriff?"

The ghostly young woman Laura had seen earlier must have waited there under the trees, avoiding the confines of the dark shed, but now she stood on the fringe of the group, watching, her eyes boring into Laura's. The accusation in her expression melted away as she looked on, something like pity taking its place. But sad longing filled her face when her gaze shifted to her husband.

Laura met Blaine's eyes and she saw his pain, not in his expression, which at that moment was wild and unhinged, but in her own mind. In the vivid images the creature poured into her brain, she saw Blaine as a young man, confused, not understanding how the woman who'd won his whole heart could simply throw it away. The brave soldier bent and broken, weeping over the scraps of shattered love.

The creature tightened its grip on Laura's middle as Blaine took a step toward them. Duke rose to his feet, unable to contain himself, creeping forward, snarling. The sheriff ordered, "Heel," and the dog dropped his head, tucking it into his shoulders, nose practically touching Blaine's leg as he worked to contain himself and stay behind his master.

Tom edged forward, the three men working each in his own way to close in on the creature quickly transforming Laura's meek, gentle uncle into something unearthly. The others were close, so close. She needed to do something to distract the demon and allow them to move in before it completely took over. Reaching for the survival knife at her waist, Laura managed to grasp it and reach down far enough to jab it into the creature's hip. It flinched. Not much and only for an instant, but just enough. She used that instant to wiggle under, and out of the vise grip. But before she could lunge away, she heard a *THWACK!*

The creature's chest sprang forward, shoving her so hard, she stumbled and went down, scrambling only a few feet before she turned to see what had happened. With its huge heaving chest still extending outward, the creature twisted, reaching back, coming up with a long red-tipped dart. It took one staggering step and another *THWACK* sounded. The beast jerked upward and turned, snarling, toward the direction where the attack had come.

There stood a man with gun raised, sighting down its barrel, and next to him, Deputy Richardson with shock registering on his face. But in the next instant both men flew backward. Adam went down, and lay still. The other man's body smashed against a tree and slid down the trunk, eyes closing as he crumpled.

The beast struggled to grab the second dart, snarling.

"Outsiders," it growled loud and harsh, apparently offended at the thought, singularly driven to torment those connected to its legendary curse, no matter how remotely. While Laura got to her feet, Blaine and Tom rushed in. Blaine grabbed the creature first, even as it deflated, turning back into her frail, tortured uncle.

The big priest shouted, "Take him down. Hold him. Don't let him go."

Blaine dropped Loy, sweeping his feet out from under him with one leg, pulling the old man toward him and down. Duke went wild, growling, barking, baring his teeth, standing feet splayed in front of Loy's face, ready to rip into the limp figure. The sheriff managed to keep the dog at bay for the time being while he pushed down on the older man's shoulders.

Tom held his ankles, but by then Loy's body had gone limp. Weeping openly, rolling his head side to side he murmured, "No, no, no." He worked to form each of his next words, "You—cane—stop—*IT*." His back arched once, then he collapsed and blacked out.

Father Gahlen swept down on one knee, raising a small bottle in one hand, prayer book open in the other—and the world turned unearthly. The air filled with an electric energy that made the hairs on Laura's arms stand on end. She felt the presence of something powerful, humbling, not free of danger, or fear, not truly safe in the normal sense but something charged with strength. Something frighteningly awe invoking encircled the group, enveloping them. It was crazy, she knew, but it seemed in that moment the very atmosphere around them glowed with an ethereal, bright haze, like a stormy sunlight.

The big priest simply bowed his head for a moment, then went to work. He shook holy water over Loy's prostrate form in the pattern of the crucifix, then laid the bottle aside. Raising the gold cross from around his neck, he canted, "In the name of the Father, and of the Son, and of the Holy Ghost. Amen. Most glorious Prince of the Heavenly Armies, St. Michael the Archangel, defend us in our battle against principalities and powers, against the rulers of this world of darkness, against the spirits of wickedness in high places."

Loy began to twitch, his body, trembling from head to foot.

The cleric lifted his eyes to Tom. "Over here, lay your hands on his head."

Blaine shifted positions with Tom as he obeyed the priest, his face grim, sweat beading on his forehead and dampening his shirt inside the open jacket he wore. On his knees, he worked his way around next to Father Gahlen.

"Pray," the priest commanded, looking at each of them in turn before he continued, "Come to the assistance of men whom God has created in His likeness and whom He has redeemed at a great price from the tyranny of the devil." He intoned, "Oh Lord, hear my prayer." Then he nodded at them to join in the response, "And let my cry come to thee."

Tom continued on in a low voice, beseeching God, repeating phrases Laura couldn't hear clearly. She knelt beside Loy, unable to speak, watching her uncle's skin ripple and his body quake. Blaine held him down the best he could, muscles now straining with the effort.

CHAPTER 32

Seconds later, Loy's possessed body contorted, back rising off the ground, shoulders pressed down. A groan escaped him, then an eerie, unearthly howl erupted from somewhere deep in his chest. His head stretched back, his neck arched, and his mouth snapped open—the sound bursting from him angry and frightened at the same time, like some volatile predator trapped, fearing for its own life—a primordial echo from the very bowels of Hell.

A dark, shadowy mist seeped from the tortured form. Rising slowly, it floated above Loy's chest, still tethered to his body. Then the black fog gathered into a shape—forming itself into the thick wolf-like body of the beast, flexing paws emerging. The creature stretched its massive bulk, the length of the man under it, clawed foot pads grinding into the earth below even as Loy shrank, returning to a beaten, broken, simple human being.

Coarse black hair became visible on the creature and a long, wet snout protruded, inches from Loy's face. Then the massive head with its pointed ears and burning red eyes, turned to survey the small group surrounding it as the creature rose above the body of her uncle and took on its own full, terrifying form. Those burning orbs finally came to rest on Laura, and it snarled.

Her chest tightened. She found herself caught between trying to draw in air and force it out. Her mind and mouth frozen, she struggled to think but no words would come. She was supposed to say something—repeat something the big priest had told her. Her mouth opened, but still nothing came out. It wanted her. It was coming for her, and she was helpless to resist. All hope and happiness sucked from her as a dark, cold abyss yawned before her eyes, and she choked on her own fear, longing to scream, unable to utter a sound.

"*In nomine Patris et Filii et Spiritus Sancti...*" Father Gahlen's deep, strong voice broke into her thoughts. "Give me your name!" Upon the priest's command Loy's body stilled. His head turned slowly, looking into the cleric's eyes. The woods went deathly silent. Nothing moved, indeed nothing breathed.

Then an eerie echoing voice came out of the man on the ground. "We are not yours to command." The eyes glaring at Father Gahlen were not Loy's. It appeared the other man was gone, until the face warped again and the agonized, terrified eyes of Laura's uncle found her, and tears slipped from the corner to run down one smudged cheek. Then slowly, as if his hand weighed too much, he reached for the bowie knife still tucked at his waist. Raising it as high as his frail arm would go, he looked away, and plunged it, with more strength than Laura would have thought possible, deep into his own belly before the beast, still poised above him, could respond.

The big priest shook his head, made the sign of the crucifix with his gold cross, but went on without skipping a beat. "I banish you from this soul. I banish you from this realm. Return to your place in Hell." His voice rose again, the words tumbling from him in a desperate rush. "In the name of the Father, and of the Son, and of the Holy Spirit." His voice fell off and he continued to mumble repeatedly in Latin, "*In nomine Patris et Filii et Spiritus Sancti.*"

"In the name of the Father, and of the Son, and of the Holy Spirit..." Laura's voice finally came of its own, in cadence with Tom's, both murmuring low.

The creature considered the battered frame of its host briefly, then cocked its head, eyeing the priest suspiciously. Its eyes darted around the group, then scanned the woods, even the air above.

"Be gone, enemy of Christ and of man. Give place to the Holy one, flee in the name of the all powerful God." The words slowing, his voice weary, the priest leaned forward and laid the gold cross on Loy's forehead, focusing on the words in the prayer book before him, ignoring the beast.

Face contorted, hate burning in its eyes, suddenly the creature threw its head back and howled. A double row of dark ridges rose along its back, tearing the beast's flesh in long slashes. In the next instant, these split and a pair of wet, silken grey wings snapped open. Flapping them with a rhythmic *whomp, whomp, whomp,* the creature rose, hovering briefly till the wings turned black—black as coal.

Then it shot straight up into the air. Rising above the trees it spiraled, higher and higher until it was a mere speck in the sky, and finally disappeared altogether. Its howl crescendoed into a blood curdling scream until all went silent again.

Time seemed to take a long, deep breath, while all of them stared into the sky. Laura almost drew a sigh of relief, but at that moment the speck reappeared, growing again, larger and more visible with each second. It came diving out of the atmosphere, hurtling straight toward them while Laura looked on helpless. Her limbs wouldn't respond.

Tom and the priest were praying the final words of a prayer together. "In the name of the Father, and of the Son, and of the Holy Spirit. Amen!"

They had both remained kneeling with heads bowed, hands on Loy's body.

The next scream Laura heard was her own. "Move! Move!" She launched herself over Loy and grabbed Tom's arm, even as Blaine lunged for Father Gahlen. They toppled backward away from Loy's body. Pitching wildly, Laura rolled and turned in time to catch sight of the creature as it slammed through Loy, down into the ground and disappeared, its final visceral howl echoing through the woods.

She stared in disbelief. There was no opening in the ground. No hole. Just a huge charred circle on the earth. Blackened, sulfurous smoke rose from the spot, but it soon dissipated, and Loy's wasted body came into view.

CHAPTER 33

Thursday, November 25, 2010

A golden brown turkey the size of an ostrich graced the center of Aunt Hattie's four-leaf dining table. The warm sweet cinnamon and nutmeg smell of apple pie combined with the savor of green beans flavored with fat-back, the odor of the onions and seasonings in the stuffing, the scent of candied sweet potatoes with marshmallows, the yeasty tang of rolls fresh from the oven, and all the other mouth-watering aromas coming from the big country kitchen set Laura's stomach grumbling.

Since the three of them were the planners and organizers of the get together, Tom, Elizabeth, and Laura decided to go through with Thanksgiving dinner despite the terrors of the previous day. Only a select few of them actually witnessed it, and *they* wanted to be together today especially, including Blaine, and Duke of course. They'd invited Father Gahlen, but the priest refused, though he'd accepted the offer of an overnight stay at Tom's.

Her brother was pouring coffee when Laura asked about the priest. Tom's hand shook a bit, and he flinched ever so slightly at the sound of the oven door banging, like a man with shell shock, but it didn't register in his voice. "I offered again, but that big man just looked..." Tom's brow creased in a pained expression.

"I'm sorry we had to involve him in this. For his sake." Silence hung thick on the kitchen aromas a moment before she added, "But I sure am glad we had him with us."

They stood that way, facing each other, each lost in their own thoughts for the moment, staring ahead. Laura pictured the big priest leaning over Loy's beleaguered form, one hand on his head, one on the gold cross, his brow sweating, praying for all he was worth.

She shook her head and sighed. "Guess I'll help get the rest of the stuff on the table."

He nodded and she turned, but just before walking away she laid a hand on his arm, and looking up, gave him a small sad smile. Tom dropped his head to stare at his feet.

Everyone had made it—Laura's daughter Tara, Tom and Elizabeth's children and grandchildren, Blaine, and even Cayley had joined them since she had no family in the area. Introductions were made and a warming, family din grew as preparations were made.

They had agreed not to ask Granny Beulah, for obvious reasons, but Tom and Elizabeth were going to break away for a while after dinner and take her a plate or two. Elizabeth would handle the visit but Tom had insisted he didn't want her going there alone, ever again.

The sheriff had taken care of the Animal Control officer and Adam immediately after things had calmed down. The explanations had taken longer with the officer than it had with his deputy. Adam had grown up with stories of the curse, like most who lived within a ten-mile radius of the hollow. It had been a small story really, compared to the varied lore and legends of these mountains, but the people here owned it, like family. Turned out having the law there at the moment things all went down made it easier to deal with in the end.

Laura hadn't had much chance to talk to Blaine yet, but Duke had been at her side most of the time since they'd arrived. The dog continued to follow close at her heels, back and forth across the kitchen to the table as she helped transfer dishes. When all were seated he laid down beside her chair, lifting his head now and then when she spoke.

Tom choked up on the blessing when he got to thanking the good Lord for everyone seated at the table, and all the friends and loved ones who couldn't be with them. To Laura's utter amazement it was Blaine who rescued the preacher.

"In the name of our Lord Jesus Christ. Amen." His deep voice was calming, solemn.

Everyone at the table echoed, "Amen."

With handfuls of treats, Tom's grandchildren finally coaxed Duke to go outside and play after dinner while Laura joined in the clean-up. The men had gone into the sitting room to watch football, but Blaine appeared beside Laura at the sink a short time later. Taking the towel from Cayley, he began drying and putting away dishes. This time Aunt Hattie didn't shoo him away.

When they finished, Blaine took her hand and with a look that melted her insides, led her out the back door. About a half mile or so later, he stepped off the trail behind a tree and cupped her chin in one hand, forcing her to look him in the eye. Then he pulled her to him and lowered his mouth to hers. She encircled his neck with both arms, giving in to the emotion, the warmth, the passion.

When he came up for air, he challenged her. "Don't ever scare me like that again."

She gave a soft laugh, and a slightly vampish smile. "Don't make me make promises I might not be able to keep." Then smile fading, she added, "I think my demons are gone. But the regrets may be harder to let go of."

She pushed back away from him and looked up into his face, unsure how to express the depth of sorrow she'd experienced picturing him broken, grieving.

He reached up and smoothed her hair, shaking his head gently, as if he knew her thoughts. "There were so many adults around you who knew, or at least had some idea of what was going on. Your father, your mother, your grandmother. You were just a child."

They stood without speaking a few moments. A woodpecker knocked on a tree not far off, a squirrel chattered a scolding warning from a limb high above. The world was back to normal. Even the wind through the trees seemed to sigh in relief, as though the pall of fear and death had been lifted. And yet, she thought she saw something—a shadow, a wisp of a yellow dress, a swirl of auburn hair. Or was it the sun playing in the trees, flashing on the leaves, flickering through the snarls and tangles of brush and vines?

Blaine rested the sides of his hands on her shoulders, cupping them around her neck, and bent down to touch his forehead to hers. For the moment both remained silent, and she let the uncertainty slide. She sensed something passing between them that words could not define. Forgiveness flowed through regrets, love mingled with doubt. Strength, or was it courage, coursed on the same tide as fear.

With an ever so slight gasp she raised her eyes to his, the emotion swelling on one of those moments of total clarity and reality, so intense, so bold, it overwhelmed Laura. She had to reach out for him, hold him, draw him into herself. He responded with a throaty sigh, both hands sliding down her back, pulling her against him, arms wrapped around her like he'd never let go.

CHAPTER 34

Friday, November 26, 2010

The house was quiet when Laura padded down the stairs. Early morning sunlight beamed across the entrance hall and into the dining kitchen, creating a bright golden path. *Follow the yellow brick road*, she thought, straight to the coffee pot. Aunt Hattie was sleeping so peacefully, Laura had quietly shut her door and tiptoed away. Laura's daughter, Tara, would probably sleep late as well, but they'd spend time together later.

Cayley hadn't arrived yet. They would need to talk. Maybe it wasn't any of Laura's business, but somehow she felt different about that kind of thing here in North Carolina. People were... well, more willing to be responsible for each other. It wasn't being nosey, it was caring, and friends and family should be about caring, shouldn't they?

The girl arrived seconds later, as if bidden by the thought. "Good morning," she spoke low and soft as she gently closed the front door and silenced her jingling keys. She entered the house subdued, setting her things on the kitchen table with a soft thump. Barely glancing at Laura, she went to the refrigerator and put the few things in it she'd brought along. Though Lord knew, they didn't need anything else, what with all the Thanksgiving leftovers.

Laura motioned to the seat across from her. "Join me in a cup of coffee? Aunt Hattie's sleeping so well, I didn't have the heart to wake her. I'll make breakfast in a little while. We'll get her up then."

Cayley sat down, clutching her coffee mug in two hands, eyes flitting from the cup to Laura's face ever so briefly.

"How long have you known about the... situation... with my uncles?" Laura bit her lip and went on, "I mean, did you already know before you came to take care of Aunt Hattie?"

The girl looked down a moment before she answered. Then she raised her head to look at Laura and said, "I grew up here. There's not many around here don't know the stories of the demon creature roaming Porter's Hollow." She paused, looking away again, appearing to consider her next words. "I've met your Uncle Curry." The girl shook her head and breathed deep. "Sorry, I don't want to speak ill of your family, but I'm *not* sorry he's gone."

"It's okay. I'm pretty sure everyone feels that way, including me." Studying the girl's face, Laura decided to press on. "You've known my brother, Tom, a while too. Haven't you?"

Cayley's cheeks colored and she stood and took her coffee cup to the sink. "Yeah, I grew up in that church, but I quit going when I was old enough to throw a fit about it. I just barely knew him before I went away, but I've been a regular ever since I came back. He's my pastor." She turned her head away and added, "And a good man."

The girl busied herself getting eggs and bacon out of the fridge, mixing the raw eggs with a bit of vanilla and milk. Then she went for the frying pans and dishes. Laura joined her, pulling out bread for toast, getting out the butter and orange juice.

"Do you mind if I ask when you left, and how long ago you came back?"

The CNA appeared to consider the question before answering. "Oh, I guess I was about seventeen. Came back when I was twenty-one. My mother was in bad health and I came to take care of her." She cut a pat of butter into the Teflon pan and turned on the burner. "She died within the year. I don't have any other family left, but my roots are here. And I like taking care of people like your Aunt Hattie. She treats you like family."

"She does that for sure."

The knock at the door startled both women. Not expecting anyone so early the day after the holiday, Laura hurried to answer, hoping Blaine had decided to check in with them.

"Howdy, Miss Laura." Adam Richardson smiled big and pulled his hat off. "I was wondering if I might have a word with Miss Cayley."

Not particularly surprised to have the young man asking after the pretty redhead, Laura stepped back, pulling the door open. "You sure can. We were just making some breakfast. We'd love to have you join us." She glanced into the kitchen at Cayley, but the girl was concentrating hard on frying bacon. "How are you this morning? You took quite a knock on the head the other day." Taking Adam's arm, Laura ushered him in and poured him a cup of coffee.

"Oh, I'm fine. Bit of a knot on the noggin', but I reckon it'll heal alright." Adam rubbed the back of his skull as he spoke. "Just glad you're okay, Miss Laura."

She merely smiled and patted his arm.

With a nod in his direction, Cayley simply said, "Morning." But the CNA definitely blushed when she greeted the deputy.

Wanting to leave the two alone for a bit, Laura announced, "I'm going to go wake up the others."

The moment for questions had passed, and in that space, Laura decided not to press the girl any further. If she were to find anything else out about what had transpired between Tom and Cayley, she'd have to go to her brother, though she wasn't sure he would be much more forthcoming. And yet, the creature had insinuated things Laura couldn't quite fathom. What could the Tom she knew, have had to do with baby killing?

The priest had warned them all not to trust everything it said. Still, she had trouble not believing it.

CHAPTER 35

Front porches, rocking chairs and mountain air, healing elixirs, or perhaps more like charms. Laura's body swayed rhythmically to and fro on the old oak rocker, putting her mind in a quiet lull. Even so, she studied the area around her—the old car garage, the shag-bark hickory beside it, the tobacco barn, the field beyond, the woods that went up the mountain beyond that—not sure what she was expecting. Signs, ghosts, demons? Fact was, the only ghosts she'd ever seen were her uncle's victims. Hopefully they were at peace now.

But, for a minute, she thought she heard the old battered four-wheeler. Her eyes searched the treeline, but just as she thought she saw something, the sound of another engine, close by, filled her ears. Blaine pulled up in his SUV, stopping in the middle of her field of vision. She leaned forward in the rocking chair, raising up, eyes returning quickly to the woods, but whatever she thought she'd seen was gone.

"Hello," his deep, soft voice caressed her, and she smiled a knowing smile. They'd had enough time Thanksgiving evening to explore their feelings for each other, and they'd come to some permanent conclusions.

He climbed the porch steps and cupped her face in one hand, leaning in to kiss her, slow. She stretched up to meet his lips, and when he lifted his head they studied each other's faces and both smiled. Then he pulled the other rocker up close and sat down beside her.

"I've had a long talk with your grandmother." He looked over at her expectantly.

Laura bit her lip and glanced away toward the woods. "And?"

"She says Loy only took Lilly's..." he stopped abruptly.

Laura reached out and laid her hand on his arm, squeezing gently.

"She claims he only did what he did to keep Curry from taking them. Said Curry had beat the tar out of him when he wouldn't tell what he'd done with them, but he never gave them up. She knew a lot more than we realized, but only recently according to her. Claimed Loy managed to communicate most of it the last time she saw him, before you and Tom and the priest came. And well, you know the rest."

"Yes, most of it, I guess."

He looked at her with brows drawn. "What do you mean? Most of it."

"The creature said things before you showed up. Accused Tom of something I'm not sure about." She shook her head. "The priest said not to believe anything it said, but there was something to it, I think. I'll have to talk to him about it."

"Hmm. Maybe it would be best to let sleeping dogs—and demons—lie."

"Maybe," she said.

"Well, in any case," he said as he stood, "I'll come by tomorrow and pick you ladies up for the funeral. Then maybe later, you and I can go to my place and..." he smiled and winked, "talk about the future some more." Then he leaned in, both hands on the arms of her rocker and kissed her long and deep.

Cayley had gone home for the day. The supper mess was cleaned up and Aunt Hattie had washed up and headed to bed early. Tara was packing and turning in early as well, since she had to leave after breakfast the next day.

The evening was quiet and Laura had no reason to be uneasy, but things still felt unfinished somehow. She was thinking of calling Tom when a car pulled up in the drive. She pulled the door curtain back to find her brother climbing the front porch steps.

Her greeting sounded subdued, even to her ears as she pulled the door open. "Hey, what brings you out here this time of night?"

"We haven't had time to talk since..." he paused awkwardly.

"Coffee's still on," she said and turned toward the kitchen, but she had an open bottle of Moscato sitting on the counter and she gestured toward it. "Unless you care to join me." She filled her glass.

"You know what?" Her brother stood back beside the table as he spoke. "I believe I will."

She looked up at him, his face white, his mouth in a thin line. "Have a seat," she said, filling a second goblet.

He took a long deep draught of the wine, then set the glass down, holding the fine stem between the interlaced fingers of his scratched and scarred hands. They'd all taken a bit of a beating in the scuffle with the creature. Physically and emotionally.

Tom sighed deep, still staring at the table, his teeth worrying his bottom lip.

"Father Gahlen warned us not to believe the thing," she offered.

When he looked up there were tears shining in his eyes.

"I know, I know, but..." he took another swig of the sweet white wine. "It's those half-truths that leave people doubting, wondering, feeling they don't know or can't trust their own family. All these years." His shoulders sagged and he sighed. "I just told Elizabeth about this. Finally." He looked Laura in the eye. "I can't have you thinking things—coming to conclusions—that maybe..."

Reaching across the vinyl tablecloth, Laura laid a hand on her brother's wrist and squeezed briefly but said nothing.

"It's not what it sounded like. Well, not entirely. I guess I am guilty of assisting in an abortion, but I didn't..." he let go of his glass and leaned back, rubbing his face with one hand. "I wasn't the father."

Unable to keep the relief out of her face, Laura gave a slight sigh. "I didn't really think so," she said.

Her brother stared hard at her, raising one eyebrow.

An inescapable blush warmed Laura's face. "Well, not really."

Tom went on, "She came to me one day when I was in the church study. She was crying, distraught. And it seemed like she was, I don't know, afraid. I mean really scared somehow. I calmed her down and she told me she was pregnant. Said she couldn't have a baby, not then. I knew she was seeing Adam Richardson at the time, so I naturally suspected he was the father. I tried to assure her he was a good boy and he'd help her. But she just started crying and insisting it wasn't possible. She never really explained her depth of distress, but she was adamant, she couldn't have *that* baby. Like maybe, I don't know, I got the feeling she'd done something with someone else, someone she feared. Or she really feared Adam would find out. I just don't know." He glanced up at Laura, guilt written in every line of his face. "I was fairly new to the pastorate, inexperienced. I wanted to help. To allay her fears. So after talking a while, I assured her I would see what I could do to find someone, some place out of town, to help her."

Laura's eyes widened, but she tried to keep her face calm, unaccusing.

He sighed again. "I arranged for an abortion clinic in Raleigh and... I paid for the procedure in advance." He lowered his gaze to the tablecloth and added, "So, I guess you could say, I'm a baby killer. Thing is, I've never told anyone, not even Elizabeth... until now."

Shivering visibly, Laura rubbed her own arms. "It must have been so difficult for you. For Cayley, too. Poor girl."

They sat in silence, both staring blankly at nothing in particular until, almost on cue, both downed the rest of their wine.

She looked up at him then. "Thanks for being there. For bringing an end to this thing."

He shook his head, derisively saying, "It wasn't me." He pushed his glass away and added, "There are powers in this world, beyond us, existing alongside of us, greater than we can explain. Powers we'd do well not to take lightly, or even boldly. I'm just glad the right ones were on our side."

"Well, I have to say, I've finally come to accept and believe in a lot of things I've often resisted." Laura recalled the moment in the woods when the air had turned eerily electric, and the hairs on her arms stood on end... that moment when something powerful entered their space, something deeply awe-inspiring, yet not quite safe.

CHAPTER 36

Saturday, November 27, 2010

Milky blind eyes stared into a grave she couldn't see. Wisps of fine white hair lifted with the breeze like downy feathers. Her back bent, knotted hand gripping the cane she rested on, Granny Beulah never shed a tear when they lowered Loy's casket into the burial pit. She stood as unmoving as she was unseeing, like the stone monuments lining the hillside that formed the Ashe County Baptist Church's cemetery.

There had been no viewing, at his mother's request. And the old bowie knife had been sealed inside the coffin with him, also Beulah's decision. Laura could only assume it was because she wanted no trace left behind of the curse that had haunted her family for so long. Granny wasn't talking to her much these days. She had allowed that Laura and Tom should come to the funeral and graveside service along with Hattie and a few others, mostly from the church, even allowed the sheriff could stand by, but she'd remained withdrawn and distant. Laura couldn't tell if it was because she was angry with them, or simply had no words to express her grief.

All at once overwhelmed with love and shared sorrow, Laura stepped forward and laid a hand on the elderly woman's shoulder. To her surprise, her grandmother leaned into her, sliding her own arm around Laura's waist. Time would do its palliative work and she would be there taking what precious moments they had left to get to know her Granny Beulah, even if some of her ways were rather strange, and even despite Tom's misgivings.

A moment later, Blaine put his arm around Laura's shoulder, and Tom's voice rose gently on the quiet hillside, "They say, '*The whole course of human history may be changed by the heart of one solitary, humble individual'*. Lord, this man was such a soul. We commend his spirit into your hands, in the name of the Father, and of the Son, and of the Holy Spirit. Amen."

EPILOGUE

A furry creature with beady black eyes, surrounded by large black fur patches, scurried out from between the boards of Beulah Porter's old garage shed as something crashed into the earth nearby. The smoke and noise drew the old raccoon's attention and it stopped, raising its snout and sniffing the air. The hair on its scruff stood up and it hissed a warning, though no one heard.

It stood erect for endless seconds. Watching. Waiting. Then from beneath its feet, the earth rose and rippled. An instant later, it growled and snorted and its body went rigid. Eyes changing to yellow, then red, its teeth bared, its face an angry snarl, it turned and ran up the mountain into the woods.

Yet the little beast had gone no more than half a mile when it came upon a large dark creature standing in its path. The transmutation didn't take long. Animals gave little or no resistance.

Not a wolf, but every bit as formidable, the huge black bear rose on its hind legs. Looming eight feet tall, it glowered over the hollow below, a long, deep growl rumbling in its chest.

Then it pivoted and lumbered up the slope, disappearing into the woods.

ABOUT THE AUTHOR

YVONNE SCHUCHART, a Nursing Assistant who once taught horseback riding lessons, has written for publication in the *York Daily Record* of York, Pennsylvania, the *Brethren Disaster Relief Auction Annual* of Lebanon, PA, and the *Lookout*, published by Standard Publishing of Cincinnati, Ohio. She enjoys writing poetry as well and has had several pieces published in various anthologies. She won the Sparrowgrass Poetry Forum's first place Award of Poetic Excellence for a piece on the loss of her son.

After raising and homeschooling all four of her other children, Yvonne decided to go to college at the tender age of forty-nine. While working full time, she obtained an AA in Social Science from Harrisburg Area Community College. She holds a certificate in creative writing from the Long Ridge Writers Group (now the

Institute for Writers), and one from the Institute of Children's Literature, which is now an affiliate of the previous association. Yvonne is a member of the Pennwriters organization, and the Alli Author Forum.

Born in Havre de Grace, Maryland, Yvonne was raised with a fundamentalist Christian background in the Free Will Baptist denomination. Her father, who told her many stories of his childhood, was born and raised in North Carolina. She draws much of her unique perspective on spiritualism from this personal history.

Yvonne now lives in the borough of Spring Grove, Pennsylvania, a community built around the paper mill established there in the 1800s. When she isn't working or writing, her 'other' life includes riding her 2011 black and chrome Harley Super Glide.

 YvonneSchuchartAuthor

 @YvonneSchuchart

 yvonne-schuchart.com

 yvonne@yvonne-schuchart.com

ALSO BY THIS AUTHOR

Book 1: *In the Shadow of Porter's Hollow*

The past catches up with us all eventually...

Haunted by murder, demon-possession and broken family bonds, can Laura Evans save her father and free her family from the demon's influence?

Book 2: *Return to Porter's Hollow*

The truth didn't set anyone free...

Troubled by paranormal visions of murder victims, Laura Evans must do whatever it takes to find her Uncle Curry if she wants to bring a murderer to justice, and save her family.

Coming Soon... *The Devil Went Down to Grassy Creek* (prequel)

and

Book 4: *Hollow Secrets*

Be first to learn when new books are released!
Sign up at yvonne-schuchart.com

Made in the USA
Middletown, DE
24 June 2023

33279767R00106